Stefano Robrotsky was born in Vienna in January, 1900 to parents who arrived in Austria after fleeing for safety from Greece during the Greko-Turkish war of 1897. His mother brought him up as best she could, helping him with his schoolwork and keeping him as well-groomed as her husband's meagre income would allow.

Stefano was exceedingly bright and excelled in three fields: Mathematics, Technical Drawing and Design and Politics. He grew up to be tall - around six feet – and slim (if a little gangly). His skin carried a natural tan, with eyes brown and hair very dark and wavy. His voice was soft and soothing to the girls who heard it, but in reality he was not a shy boy!

1

Reuben, his father, had brought his wife to Vienna, Austria to escape the communist movement in Hungary. He settled in quickly, working for the Church as a vicar. His low income gave them an assisted property to live in. Not being particularly motivated to climb the ladder within the Church, he was a bit of a disappointment to his wife. His political views were quite extreme as he mixed more and more with a young, politically motivated lad by the name of Adolf.

Stefano's father wanted the best for his son and was happy to do without in order that he got the best chance in life. He taught him to play the piano exceptionally well and made sure his religious beliefs followed his own.

As Stefano went through the education system, his academic abilities were noticed more and more by his tutors. Hopes were raised as his results from examinations were seen to be exceptional. Applications were made to the Universities of Oxford and Cambridge in the UK as well as Harvard in the United States of America. A scholarship or at least an assisted position was agreed and as he turned eighteen years old he left Austria and arrived at Kings College, Oxford.

English at first was a problem, but he soon settled in and excelled at reading Mathematics. He progressed through his three years there and exited with an honours degree. While he had been studying Maths, his passion for Engineering had remained. He had mixed well with his peers and now he could converse in English with no detectable accent. From here he went on to read Engineering and Design at Harvard. The three years passed quickly and again he came out with an honours degree.

He always remained a bit of a loner, joining in with social groups but never really getting involved. He mixed with many females but never really got involved on a passionate basis. All relationships were on his terms: they started when he chose and ended as he chose. He knew his voice was rather harmonious to many young women and he made sure he took advantage of this asset at all times, leaving many distressed ladies on either side of the salty pond.

Once his studies were finished, Stefano looked at the offers that came in for work from British and American companies through the old school network. He quickly found his way into the Civil Service and allowed his prowess in Mathematics, Economics and Engineering to show. The establishment above him loved his enthusiasm and once they saw he could converse fluently in German, both oral and written, he was recruited into a deeper layer of government business.

As things progressed, he kept his private life very separate from his personal. Being seen as a person who kept himself to himself and with no known family, he was recruited and thrust deeper into the Whitehall establishment. He had instinctively changed his mode of communication with his father and mother months earlier, advising them that his work kept him on the move and giving them Post

Office or hotel addresses he would be at in the near future.

As time went by, he was sent on trade missions to Germany under the guise of representing various British companies. While the other company representatives who travelled with him tried to sell their wares, Stefano was assessing the changes in Germany under her new lord and master. His instructions were to investigate and assess exactly what Mr. Hitler was doing and what treaties he might be breaking. Young Robrotsky was hatching his own ideas as he saw the German military might grow. Always one for himself, he was not going to let an opportunity like this go to waste.

He let it slip that it would not be too much to ask him to take a risk or two, and soon it was requested by his superiors that he relocate to Germany. His mission: to take on a job a little below his station and work his way up through the system as a mole. If war was to come, he would be an invaluable asset to the Allies, as well as being paid rather well. He took the training and was off on the next chapter of his life.

*

It was 1932, and his father had been writing to Stefano, suggesting he should come back to Austria. His friend Adolf had become a great man in his father's view and there would be good work under him in Economics! It was seven years since Stefano had been home to see his parents and he thought it would be a good move to go back to Vienna, and then on to Berlin.

On returning to Vienna he found many things had changed: his mother was quite withdrawn and almost subservient to his father. His father, although still with the Church, had become very politically motivated in following the word of *Mein Kampf,* written by his friend Adolf; his views were no longer charitable toward the Jewish population. The Brown Shirts had taken over, but Stefano's father was still able to open many doors very quickly for his son. All of this made Stefano's British superiors very happy.

Stefano found work within the Austrian Government and was quickly drawn into new ideas being pushed forward. As Austria and Germany became united, he was transferred to Berlin and became very close to the Nazi Party. Although he did not agree personally with a lot of the views of the time, he was quickly becoming a rich man working for the Party. His social life was as he wanted it: if he wanted, it was provided; when he was finished, it was taken away. This suited the cold-hearted, double paid bastard; as far as he was concerned, life was good!

He understood British and American ways exceptionally well; he could advise fairly accurately what their next move would be. This meant he became well trusted and he advanced quickly. At the same time the Brits loved his advancement and enjoyed the feedback he gave them.

Time passed quickly, as did Stefano's advancement through the tiers of the establishment. As the German invasion of Poland surged ahead - and then the

English declared War on Germany - he realised there was a role for him within the military. As Germany's relatively unchallenged progress across Europe continued, he was transferred to Amsterdam to oversee the Management and Engineering problems of lowland Holland. Looking after the flood defences and shipping, he quickly became bored and requested a more challenging role. It was at this point he realised what he excelled at: he became an investigative hunter, chasing down all the money and savings that the Party could acquire. It meant finding legal papers; documents and evidence of past earnings; property and family history - then finding and providing legal ways of stripping these assets from the owner. This then progressed into hunting those of the Jewish religion and

- once all their assets had been 'processed' - deporting them. It was not long before Stefano became known as the 'Jew Hunter'. Living like a king with many staff, he chased down every piece of wealth he could. Not being too greedy for himself, all went well for him. He always stayed behind a desk, using subordinates to do his bidding and hedging his bets on the long term outcome of the war.

By 1943, Stefano was one of the most feared men in Holland. Highly trained as he was, he understood by then that the Allies were going to win the war and he was going to have to come up with a plan for his future. Firstly, he started to take a much larger share of the wealth he was stripping from the Dutch people.

The accounts showed that things were getting tighter as it was becoming harder to find those of the Jewish faith to - in truth - steal from. Actually he had started to use a few men, who were loyal to him and his money, to chase down and frighten the last of the Jewish left in hiding into running. His team would provide a potential escape route as sympathisers and trick their victims into breaking cover. Bless them, they ran like sheep, straight into traps, where there was nowhere to run. They would be shot en masse and Stefano's men would then wade in and retrieve all their belongings. The proceeds went into his private banking facilities. His wealth grew to extraordinary heights, mainly in gold and precious stones.

As D-Day arrived, Stefano began to activate his escape plans. Firstly all his trusted men never got the opportunity to talk; he made sure they never took another breath. He had kept his face out of the limelight for a year or two to decrease the chance of being recognised when the time came to run.

Using his papers to cross Holland, he moved to Belgium and went underground, ditching all that could identify him and laying low. As the British and Canadians advanced and the Nazis were pushed back, he rose up to be counted. Claiming to be British, with that well-polished accent he was accepted quickly. When asked for a name he gave them the name 'Steve Robinson'. In the hectic last weeks and days of the war, he quickly dissolved into the background and was forgotten by the forces that were furiously fighting their way towards Germany.

During this time Stefano took on a second in command: Miss Urdanne, a short, slim, mousy haired woman who had worked for the SD and Gestapo in Paris up to just a few months ago. Her speciality was making sure men either told her what she wanted to know, or did exactly as they were instructed. At this she could possibly be more ruthless than Robinson, as he was now known. The ideal combination: a greedy, power hungry man with an assistant who never took 'no' for an answer!

'Stephen Robinson' now started to look for a way to make his fortune legitimate. With his economic background he soon realised shipping and oil were going to be the game of the future. Moving to

Rotterdam, he looked for opportunities. This came in buying Liberty ships from the United States and starting to ship goods, buying non-perishable goods around the world and shipping them to ports where rebuilding was being undertaken. Over the next five years his empire grew and by 1949 he was an unbelievably wealthy man.

Robinson had observed in the newspapers that many of the war crime trials were being held in the Haig. He was now beginning to realise there were Jewish survivors from the concentration camps who were appearing out of Tel Aviv and Israel – and that they might be looking for him. He had to come up with a plan. Too vain for surgery, he needed a retreat far enough away from the areas where he had worked during the war to run his business empire without being overlooked or observed too closely. The search resulted in securing the ownership of a small island not too far from Turkey in the Mediterranean.

He now started to recruit a slightly different kind of personnel from the normal deck crew, engineers and officers. On one of his vessels, the woman who had worked privately for the Gestapo and who was now going by the name of 'Ciao Bella' ('Goodbye Love') was overseeing all operations. The ship would sail every three months to Accra on the coast of Ghana to pick up minerals and hardwood. Ciao Bella would offer work to up to fifty or so local men and take them on board, offering better than local wages as well as free lodging. They would be returning in three months and so should arrive home relatively

wealthy. The men would be filtered prior to embarkation; any who looked a little less than one hundred percent fit would be rejected on health grounds – but duties on board were relatively light.

Within the ship's hold were a furnace and acid baths, and ore containing gold that another vessel had picked up from South Africa. Mercury was used to leech the gold out of the ore. This would then be separated through a process overseen by Ciao Bella, the gold being smelted down into small ingots for storage and trading. Silver coins that had been legitimately purchased from banks around the world were sorted. Any coins with known high contents of silver were dropped into the acid baths. The silver was separated out from the base metals and recovered. The coins with low silver content were returned to banks through legitimate businesses. The Ghanaian men suffered considerable lung damage from mercury poisoning and the toxic gas from the acid baths.

The ship would make firstly for Robinson's private island, where the gold and other valuables would be discharged. The Ghanaian men would also disembark for the opportunity of rest and recuperation. They were offered medical help from Robinson's well-equipped medical centre. All services were offered in exchange for a signed chit. At that time each chit represented a number of days of work. In reality, according to international law, these men became slaves!

When these men became too weak to work or inefficient at their tasks, they would be moved around to different jobs. Eventually after six months or so they would be offered the return trip to their homeland. They would be paid, and they would board the homeward bound ship enthusiastically. During the trip they would be expected to work as usual, but once the vessel was past Morocco and heading south on the Atlantic Ocean, they would be brought up on deck, checked for anything of value - and shot without mercy. Ciao Bella then would slit and hack them open from the throat down to the pubis bone, and roll what was left overboard as dusk fell. The blood in the water quickly attracted sharks and the like to feast on these poor mutilated men. The bodies did not last long enough in the water for those on passing vessels to see any remains, and so no questions were ever asked.

The wives of the enslaved Ghanaian men wondered when their men would be coming home. When the ship their men had left on returned to dock, the women would clamour for attention. They would be pushed aside and given a little local currency to calm them, then told that their men had stayed on for several more months, as the rate of pay was so good. On each trip, while this was happening, another fifty or so new men were recruited and shipped away with another cargo.

While these men were being abused as slaves, employed on the island in construction duties, the same vessel would depart with a regular crew. With every appearance of respectability and honest trade, the ship's first destination would be India, where a much greater price could be realised for the precious metals. Ciao Bella would stay and oversee operations on the island as Robinson's right hand, while the smelting ship ran normal, legitimate routes.

On the east side of the island, a grand excavation was being dug by hand, with pick and shovel, out of the rock. As things progressed, dynamite and small excavators were used. Eventually the rock that came out of the island was shipped away and sold as road aggregate to Italy and France to help rebuild the ruined roads and cities after the war.

During this time, Robinson ran his shipping line himself; his crews were efficient, loyal and well paid - all was legitimate. The captains, when they required it, were allowed to find free cargo to add to the manifest and so increase revenue. As the captains paid the shipping agents well and the dockers' unions even better, seamen often jumped other anchored vessels to berths to get much faster turn-around. This made the line even more profitable. Robinson imported different equipment, steels and building materials from all over the world to build his future on his private island.

At the same time he often travelled quite openly, taking official trips to open up shipping opportunities and build client relationships. These trips took him to the USSR and the USA as well as all over Europe. With his wealth he bought into the Californian oil fields at Long Beach. He knew that black gold was going to be the most important resource in the world. Although the American oil fields were producing well for their domestic market, the Middle East - controlled before World War II mainly by the British - was rapidly becoming the largest producer.

Nobody took any notice of Robinson's empire.

It was still growing at an extraordinary rate.

Chapter 1: Things of Interest

Soaking up the early evening sunshine. Wearing her now dried-out navy bikini, a lilac shawl draped over one shoulder. Crystal blue eyes hidden behind the fashionable sunglasses, Murtyl picked up her glass and took a sip of the golden liquid. She lit a cheroot and glanced down at Berty.

"I either need to be racing and joining in the fun, or we need to be finding something to do. Reporting on the Mille Miglia is just frustrating; we're half way through the race, in beautiful Brescia and I've had enough. What do you think, Berty? Check the finances with Charles in France and see what can be done. We've done a few little jobs on the side and the finances should stretch to a full professional season."

With his southern French accent Berty replied, "I understand, but we only just got out of the last job five weeks ago, and that was by the skin of our teeth. You can't push the adrenalin button all the time. While The Times is bankrolling you to socialise with the cream of the crop of the racers, why not just enjoy the season? We both know the work you want is going to find you and a telegram will appear soon enough."

At that Murtyl stood up and raised her sunglasses. She winked at Berty, while nodding towards the Grand Hotel. "If you're still fit enough, we have an hour before dinner to kill!' She strolled away with that slight swing to her hips, through the bistro area towards the hotel, glancing down and rotating her left forearm to look at the face of her 1947 Rolex Oyster with the luminous hands, strapped to her elegant wrist.

She nodded to admiring men as she passed them by. All the ladies glanced at her with that 'if only I had that kind of style, that confidence, the world I live in would surely be different' look. The men watched her glide by with that look in their eyes that said, "Whoever or whatever the creator or God is; no matter how hard they try; nothing is ever going to surpass the poise, simplicity and uncomplicated beauty that has just burnt an image never to be forgotten into my cerebral cortex and retinas." The ladies looking down at their tables, shuffled and moved glasses to regain their individual gent's attention. Racing cars drove by on their way back from the service area and back to Parc fermé, but they may as well have been silent. Nobody noticed.

Just as things were about to return to normal and the sound of mixed conversations were starting again, Berty strolled through. His unfashionably long blond wavy hair and naturally sculpted body did almost the same to the girls as Murtyl had done to the boys.

As evening drew in, they readied for dinner. Berty wore a blue-white, pressed cotton shirt. Once he had the buttons done up, Murtyl tied his bow tie for him and then, after he had pulled his dinner jacket over those broad shoulders, made sure it was straight. She ran her hands over his chest to straighten the jacket out and looked into his eyes. "You do know I'm serious. If I don't find some action soon, I'll get us into trouble. We're going to have to find some."

Closing the clasp on her diamond necklace from behind, Berty thought about it. He ran his hands gently over her shoulders then down her sides, admiring the black silk dress she wore that hid a body that was defined, toned and wore no visible underwear.

He said, "Dinner now. You have drivers to entertain and talk to. The Times is expecting you to do your job the way you always do it. When the thousand kilometre race is over, we can talk to the boys and look at some possibilities. In the meantime, why not telegram old Flem and see if he has anything up his sleeve? He is probably the only one who has not used you since the war, even though he is officially your employer."

"You may be right; when this bloody race is over we shall talk. I have a dead two weeks. But I don't think we should get used to calling Mr. Fleming 'Flem'. If he gets wind of it, I may get a rapped knuckle or two."

She laughed and asked if Berty had been working on anything different that might be of help in the future, or at least fun to know about now.

As dinner with some of the drivers came to an end, Berty pulled out a pencil and started to draw on a napkin. "I've been working on this kite thing in my head for a while now and I think it is time to build and test it. I posted some drawings to Charley a few weeks ago; he should have acquired most of the materials by now."

Murtyl replied, "So you haven't been totally relaxing then - and which of the chambermaids are you playing with during the day when I'm out in the sun working?" She laughed as she knew he would never let her down; he loved her in every form that is possible, although they would never be lovers again. He was free to exercise his physical prowess when and wherever he chose, as she was. Their bond, from childhood through to today, meant they felt each other's pain; knew each other's moves and would always be a team.

The next day she interviewed the winner of the 1951 Mille Miglia 405, driven and navigated by Villoresi and Cassani - who had brilliantly taken his Ferrari 340

America Vignale Berlinetta, entered by the Scuderia Ferrari works team, round the one thousand kilometre course in twelve hours, fifty minutes and eight seconds. He had averaged almost seventy five kilometres per hour, including fuel stops, over unbelievably narrow country roads, dirt tracks and cobbles, through city centres and country villages. They had done a magnificent job in the works Ferrari. There were hardly any British drivers and only one finishing British car of note, driven by Healey and Healey in a Nash-Healey 3850 who finished thirtieth in the Mille Miglia 406. Murtyl struggled to find an excuse to interview the pair and was just bored with the whole circus. She grudgingly described the course and the racing, but struggled to understand why the readers of the motor sports section in The

Times would be interested, as there was no real UK interest. Maybe things of interest would pick up in a few weeks at the next Grand Prix.

In the meantime she and Berty would get back to Dole in France, work out, stay fit, hone their skills and build with Charley this kite thing that Berty had drawn on the napkin.

She just needed to be challenged.

*

The year before, PB Industries in the UK had won part of the fabrication contract for the Obninsk Nuclear Power Plant that was to go on line producing power to the Russian Electricity Grid on June 27th, 1954. The project was a design and build joint venture between the British and the Russian Government. As ever, the British were happy to assist somebody else in taking the risk, but still reap the benefits if the project proved successful, while avoiding the embarrassment of potential failure. Most of the Engineering companies in the UK that would normally have gone for a large UK government contract had stepped out of the tendering process early in fear of being involved in a project that had such a high potential risk. It was a power source that might not be totally understood and as such, it was just a little too risky. After all there was still work to be done rebuilding Europe after that dashed awful war.

It had been only six years before that the United States Army had detonated the 'Gadget' at the Trinity Atomic Bomb Site near Socorro, New Mexico. The test was an implosion-design plutonium device which when detonated released an energy burst equivalent to twenty kilotons of TNT. It was one big bang, to coin a phrase. This device was identical to the 'Fat Man' and 'Thin Boy' bombs dropped on Hiroshima and, less than a month later, on Nagasaki with devastating consequences. In truth nobody really knew how hazardous radioactive isotopes could be. Mathematically half-lives were understood but true comprehension was way, way, in the future for scientists.

PB Industries got on with their contract, producing the reactor and cooling systems ready for shipping to the construction site. The British scientists and government officials watched over every part of the construction, continuously checking and testing the quality of materials and their fabrication. As a company, PB Industries made no mistakes; it was run essentially by good businessmen, employing a lot of specialist skills from all over Europe. As many of these employees were actually refugees without a home, PB Industries had built an area of dwellings on a secure site for them. Most had come from Germany and were highly educated industrial workers, who hoped to earn good money then return home to help with the rebuilding of their own country. Language was not a problem as most of the work was down to technical drawings, the understanding, and executing of this instruction. As no nuclear testing was to be done on site, radiation was never an issue, but cleanliness was.

The British Government was very proud of this partnership with Russia and the construction that PB Industries had undertaken. Whenever the project was failing or falling behind schedule, the bean counters found more pounds to propel the assignment forward. No questions were ever asked about wasted material, excessive man-hours or equipment needing to be renewed. This was to be the world's first fission power reactor plant and they just were not going to be the part of the team that was late to the party or fail to get there. But all the time materials were being spirited away by a smaller, duplicate team producing a smaller but nevertheless exact copy of the reactor being built. PB Industries did have duplicates of the rest of the construction plans that the reactor was to couple up to and were actively working on that too - just somewhere else!

The man overseeing the two operations was a great front man, big in stature, broad across the shoulders and a former Yorkshire rugby player. He had dominated the pack with his enthusiasm and bulk. Dr. Peter Blyth was English and had had a tough war from behind a desk, making decisions that most men could not. His organisational skills were of the highest quality and he danced rings around the British officials. He always had a good reason why more money was required, why materials had been found to be faulty and why more and more of the build should be done in-house, rather than letting other companies supply anything. This smoke screen allowed the smaller duplicate to be completed earlier than the contracted system. It was spirited away from the works to a shipping company and smuggled out of the UK. Dr. Blyth had been at Cambridge with a certain Steve Robinson pre-war and now, post 1946, they were building this company quickly.

New welding skills were developed during construction, to deal with the new metals that were being supplied to site to match the requirements of the design. The dangers of nuclear power generation were not fully understood, but a belt and braces approach was being adopted for the world's first reactor. This joint venture for the British and the Russians could simply not be allowed to go wrong. To be a world leader you simply had to prove you were both a leader and the best. There was no way the

British could ever hope to be a world power again unless it was through technology.

During this period the old Nazi submarine pens at Brest, leading out to the Atlantic from the coast of France, were leased from the French Government by a growing shipping concern. SR Industries' Liberty ships were slow and relatively small, just fitting into these pens. Every few months one of these vessels would come in to be dry docked and refitted. The hull would be scraped clean and painted in the owner's colours. The engine rooms were stripped and converted to diesel power engines driving giant electrical generators, which in turn drove the motors that drove the screw through its gearbox. While this work was being carried out, one of the cargo holds, roughly midships, was converted too.

The conversion was to allow a pre-constructed unit to be fitted in just a few hours when loading cargo at Teesport in the UK.

The units to be fitted to the new brackets and holders were sixty foot long, dead straight tubular items. Each tube was slanted forward along the line of the vessel from the base of the cargo hold so that only the top foot or so was visible above the deck. To all intents and purposes it looked like a vent to allow the hold to breathe when the hatches were down but which could be sealed in rough weather. The tubes were about ten inches in diameter with a cushioning hydraulic dampening system at the bottom, which in turn sat on a massive strengthening plate attached to the hull. They were coated in a dark paint and above the dampening mechanism was a large steel closable opening port into the tube. This tube was probably fifty percent wider in diameter than the tube above, into which the upper tube seemed to be inserted a good way but was fixed rigidly to the hull. Above the steel opening breech-like mechanism attached to the narrower tube were inverted 'Y' structures roughly every ten feet or so up the tube. Each of the Y legs was capped with a small opening mechanism. At their end were wires that came out and ran in individual pairs back to a control room. Prior to this being fitted in at Smith's Dock on the River Tees, all sorts of wiring had been put in place in the pens, including an office-like structure with direct communication to the bridge and the shipping line owner.

Once all this was fitted and wired, an inner hold that had been put in place in Brest was now resealed, leaving what looked like a normal hold. It just happened to be a little smaller than the others on the vessel.

Enough room, ventilation systems and working space was hidden within this structure for seven men to work together comfortably. Direct access to the vessel's superstructure and communications were all installed and connected. The vessel would load with steel over these few days and be off to her new destination. As she was carrying steel from the 'Steel River', as the Tees was known, adjustments to the holds were normal. Customs remained sleepy and watched these vessels come and go on their round trips. Iron ore from Canada arriving for the steel works at Redcar was unloaded, holds swept clean and worked steel of various quality in pipes, girder and plate loaded for export. Everything quite as it should be!

Chapter 2: A Suitcase Glider

Berty and Murtyl had left Italy and driven following the Riviera to Monaco. They stayed a few nights to mix with some of the well-to-do and generally have a look around. The owners of the La Rascasse Café bar, who had developed a relationship with the couple when Murtyl had been reporting on the Monaco Grand Prix, greeted them as long-term friends. The world famous café had no rooms for hire but the two were allowed to stay upstairs during the odd evenings they were in town. During the day they swam and sunbathed off the pier or in the famous swimming pool. At night they went out to eat and came back to La Rascasse for drinks and to rest. Business was never discussed until they set off towards Lyon and back to Dole, in their not too old Citroën Travant, the good old reliable car that handled so well and which had saved so many lives of the Resistance during World War II. Its size belied its agility and strength; the lines were smooth and efficiency was superb. This was an inconspicuous car that was designed to do a job well and without falter. It was easy to repair and fast if required - just as Murtyl liked it!

Once settled in at Dole with Charles, they trained by day: an hour or two of light repetition and toning exercise; lunch, then on with some weaponry practice. For Berty, this consisted of home-made catapults with wrist braces to allow extra power by taking the strain on the wrist back to the forearm.

Using 2.2mm ball bearings power was not a problem, but at more than forty feet accuracy was an issue. Murtyl practised drawing and throwing small knives at moving targets and then they moved on to Judo and Aikido in their training complex. Charles watched in awe at the way the two went at it, advising on Feints and the Disguising Intent and how to use the opponent's energy efficiently to assist your own moves to achieve the desired results; turning the opponent's advantage to disadvantage. His knowledge from his travels in martial arts before joining the monastery was, as ever, impressive - especially for a pacifist.

When there was no particular reason to travel with Murtyl, Berty lived here at the hidden part of the monastery. Charles's superiors knew nothing of the complex that had been developed during the war and expanded to be used as it was now.

Charles was on a light leash with the abbot, even though he missed the majority of his duties and prayer times. This light touch was for several reasons: firstly, Charles's family, often for no apparent reason, donated a lot of money – and this really *was* a lot - to the Priesthood. Secondly, Charles was always on hand with his herbs, acupuncture, muscle 'things' and all sorts of tricks that kept all the other monks on their feet. He also seemed to be incredibly good at maintaining all equipment and buildings.

When Murtyl was away they kept fit. Even though Charles would never leave the estate, he worked with Berty, training, practising and developing skills, designing and building new equipment and keeping up with anything new. They were both aware that Murtyl's life could depend on it, and both their lives would not be the same without her.

On this occasion, Charles had been able to find enough parachute silk to construct Berty's idea for a kite, using light, fine tubular steel of various sizes. He had purchased pipe bending equipment, oxy-acetylene and various weights of steel wire ropes with eyelets to suit. It took a day or two for them both to be happy with the frame. It was a large, sharp-ended fifty degree triangle with a centre spar, lightly braced then made rigid with a vertical bar that was braced to the frame by the tensioned wires. Every eighteen inches or so, the tubular steel decreased in size so that each of the lengths of pipe slid inside the next like a Russian doll. The whole structure would fit inside a large briefcase and could be erected in seven minutes. The hard part was fixing the silk and finding out if the idea was viable. But, they reasoned, if the new jet-propelled Vulcan bomber was off the ground, surely this would work!

Clipped solidly to the centre of the frame, but slightly ahead of the centre of gravity, was a three-part triangular shape that was to act as a control. When constructed, at the point of centre of gravity, there was to all intents and purposes, a sling supporting a canvas sheet to act as seating for the controller.

For the first time, helping Charles with this contraption, Berty had his doubts.

He knew nothing of the Vulcan test flights over near Manchester and, now that it was constructed, the glider looked to him rather like a very large and flimsy paper aeroplane.

Murtyl was helping now and had been asking about lift and leading edges; the possibility of prolonged flight and distances achievable.

Berty just looked at her and stated in his French accent, "Rising air, height, forward motion offers lift. This is a suitcase glider; we just have to learn the rules and learn to fly without ego or power. Tomorrow we go to a quiet hillside with wind running up her and start to learn to fly all over again."

Murtyl smiled quietly to herself as she turned, walking away in her sweat-soaked gym clothes and shaking her head.

She thought quietly to herself, "What the hell has that genius dreamt up now? Is it my neck or his, first flight? As she walked past their firing range, she picked up a knife and threw it in the dim light. It left her right hand at fantastic velocity, her throwing action coming all the way from the balls of her feet as she flexed through the ankles, knees, hips and torso, culminating in a flick through her arm and wrist that sent the knife at lighting speed. Over fifty feet it flew, its rise and fall in an arc that was not more than three inches. It landed blade first in the intended target, sinking deep into the hard wooden shape of a man four foot tall and with a white marker where the heart would have been. Her steel blue eyes sparkled in the dim light. Satisfied, she slapped the frame of the door as she went through and headed off for a well-earned hot steamy shower and then sleep.

As dawn broke, the three of them were off in the Travant to some local slopes near vineyards. The banks were south facing and as the sun began to shine hard on these gentle slopes, the air began to flow up them. They unpacked the briefcase and quickly erected the frame. They attached the silk with a few stiffening batons inserted and looked at each other. Berty and Murtyl both wanted to be first to try and fly this thing.

Berty drew out his faithful double-sided coin, tossed it in the air and called, "Heads!" He caught it in his right hand and placed it on the back of his left hand. The two sides were tails and Murtyl had won again; Berty knew it was better to support her from the ground, where his weight could be advantageous.

Murtyl put on her leather flying hat, goggles and throat mic connected to a small transmitter and receiver and in turn a battery. A small base station was built into the back of the Travant as a relay and booster station to the identical equipment Berty wore; Charles could listen.

Berty tied a light but strong thin wire rope to the Travant, looping it round a feeder bar, attaching the other end to a steel ring looped through the back of Murtyl's belt at the rear. He then let out not more than twenty five feet of rope between himself and her and looped the wire across his back. She wore old Land Girls' clothing as she needed the freedom of movement. They discussed the probable principles of flying the contraption as the breeze grew. She then stood under the contraption with the canvas and rope seat behind her and the control bar in front of her. Berty's hands were encased in thick leather gloves and he guided the wire around his body from the front at either side. His jacket was made of thick woven wool, offering a little friction and some protection in case the wind took the kite violently. He played the wire out and heaved it back in as required, to help Murtyl. She then walked forward, lifting the nose into the air one or two degrees at a time. Within a few minutes her feet were inches off the ground and she was able to hover with confidence, then slip sideways from left to right and from right to left. The control was instinctive and she struggled to explain the flight characteristics to Berty over the radio.

After a few rough landings, laughs and bruises, the tether was played out further and further, until eventually she soared away in complete control, relaying all she felt to Berty to make his first flights as easy as possible. This contraption must have a future!

But what the hell that future was, was anybody's guess.

Chapter 3: Land Girl

The spring morning sunshine warms the back of the curtains, raising the temperature in little Phillipa's bedroom. The spring birds are chirruping outside the open window, slowly bringing her to life from her deep sleep. She comes fully awake and clambers from her bed, rubbing the sleep from her eyes. Her yellow nightgown matches the curtains, which she draws slowly back to reveal a cloudless bright blue sky. The trees are hardly moving as there is no discernible breeze.

It's seven thirty on a Saturday morning; wondering what the new day may have in store for her, she brushes her teeth and washes and rinses her face, drying it with a towel. Then all four feet nine inches of her glides to her wardrobe. She pulls out a matching dressing grown then sits and brushes her hair, whilst watching squirrels dance through the trees. At nearly ten years old she feels all grown up.

Once her hair is brushed and she is satisfied that all looks as it should, she makes her way to the kitchen. On the way her little feet glide into a blue pair of slippers with little rabbits' ears sewn on.

She fills the kettle and switches it on; reaches for mugs out of the cupboard - the one with 'Dad's Little Helper' on the side is her favourite - and her father's best pint mug.

"Yorkshire tea we have, Yorkshire tea it is. Yorkshire born, Yorkshire bred, strong in't 'arm and thick in't 'ead," she mumbles to herself, giggling. She places some white thick-sliced bread in the toaster, flicks the switch, and goes to check the mail. Yes, the postman's been and the mail is retrieved from the doormat. She checks through the mail to see whether anything could be for her. No, just the usual stuff for Dad. Nothing she can see that looks exciting. She returns to the kitchen; the tea is made and the toast buttered, fresh black pepper ground over it. Just as she and Dad like it. All is then placed on a tray, and up the stairs she treads, very carefully so as not to spill anything. Once outside her father's bedroom door, she places the tray on the floor.

A little knock on the door with her tiny knuckles and the question is asked: "Dad, are you nearly awake yet?" Nothing is heard in return, so she tries again, the knock a little louder on the Ledge and Brace oak door: "Dad - are you nearly awake yet?"

The answer from behind the door comes back: "Sorry Sweetheart, I was miles away. Come on in and we can discuss what's planned for today."

As she opens the door and picks up the tray, her father, Nick, sees what Phillipa has been up to and frowns. "Thank you my little angel but you know you should not be touching hot things in the kitchen unless I'm there."

"Yes Dad, I understand that but I needed a cup of tea and you're still in bed. So you can shut up and enjoy it, or I can take it back downstairs, and you can get up! Anyway, why are you still in bed? The sun's up and the day's already half over! There's an engine to build in the garage and it won't build itself. We both know if you're the only part of the build that's late, the lads won't be happy. Murtyl would kill you, and above all I would be embarrassed."

"Holy poop scoops young lady, you're ten going on a nagging fifty! If Murtyl had ever had a daughter, you sure as hell would fit the bill. How many times have you gone through that diary of hers?"

"Oh, a few dozen times. I know it nearly off by heart. Do you realise how special she was, Dad?"

"Sweetheart, you have no idea. In fact the reason why I was first loser this morning in getting up is that I was late to bed last night. I went to buy a sherbet next door at the pub – I meant to just sit outside for ten minutes then come back home. I left the beer on the bar and came home for my notebook and started to recall a few things. I think a news item on the telly must have triggered something in my head, and I had that ringing in my ear again. I have a feeling that, just maybe, the next diary is going to appear."

"Oh Dad, how exciting! Will you let me help you with the research as you go through it and verify it?"

"Blinking right I will, all hands to the pumps when that turns up. The publisher for *First Tears* keeps asking for the next diary, and I can never give him a satisfactory answer. Ron Kirk never gives me a clue when I see him, the wily old fox, even if I offer him a coffee. I suppose he has to stick to his word and contract though. A tip-top chap, all the same."

"So Dad, can I read your notes? You know I like to see what you were like when you were a little less prehistoric than you are now. I like to think of you as good caveman material in the morning when you haven't shaved!"

"You cheeky little madam. When this tea and toast is gone, I'll get up, shave and shower, and we can get on with that engine. And if you can guess the emotion I felt, on the day I was making notes about last night, I'll go through it with you after tea this evening."

"That's fine Dad, spit-n-shake." Her little hand darts out, travelling at high velocity past her mouth, there is the sound of spitting then it is there ready to shake her dad's hand - and all before he can raise his own hand.

The deal is done! Off <u>Phi</u>llipa goes, to get dressed in her little white dungaree working overalls. Her red and white patterned headscarf is tied around her head, holding up her long, silky hair. A little leather belt around her waist keeps things neat and tidy; she looks all grown up - just like a Land Girl from the forties. She goes out through the back door and opens up the garage. By the time Dad is outside and entering the garage, the workbench has been cleared and wiped down. The tools for the day are out and clean; the clean rag box is to the right of the bench and the box for old broken parts and recyclable stuff is to the left. Her little bright green eyes have missed nothing as usual. The packages from the week's post with new oil seals; gaskets and the like are set at the back of the bench, ready to be used. The oil can and grease are there too. Nick looks at his pride and joy, dressed in her overalls, and wonders how she can be so organised; it is beyond him! Maybe she really is taking Murtyl's diary to heart. She is efficient, tireless, determined and ridiculously cheeky - or is that just forthright? Anyway, enough thinking. Time we got on with the job.

Last Sunday, together they had fitted the reground crankshaft to the 'A' series engine. The flywheel was on and all was torqued up. Today's task is to fit the four new Hepolite pistons into the re-bored cylinders with a pair of new piston rings and an oil scraper ring to each piston. The gudgeon pins are pressed through the pistons and little ends as an interference fit first, and then they are weighed with the short pinned connecting rods. Each part has to be weighed and then matched up so that when placed together, a piston, its rings, a gudgeon pin and connecting rod when assembled are the same as each other in weight. This is blueprinting and balancing of the engine during the build. It will allow the little engine to rev higher. With a well-ported cylinder head, the right camshaft, carburettion, exhaust and ignition it will produce considerably more power. One hundred and thirty five horses is the aim for this little 1298cc classic. With the blueprinting it should rev happily to seven thousand, six hundred revolutions per minute - nearly twenty five percent higher than the original designer's specification! Now, one at time, a connecting rod is dropped down through a bore, followed by its piston. Once the piston is down the bore as far as the scraper ring, a piston ring compressor is used to hold the rings tight to the piston. The piston is then pushed into the bore until the bottom of the connecting rod meets up with the crankshaft. It is quite messy as everything is oiled prior to assembly. Now the big end shell bearings are inserted and the cup fitted. The motor is turned over to make sure things move freely. The big end bolts are tightened slowly, always keeping a check that everything carries on moving freely. The bolts are eventually torqued up and the locking washer tabs knocked over to secure the nuts.

At all times they remember: cleanliness is next to godliness. As the four pistons are fitted, tested and capped off,

Phillipa makes notes, handing parts to her father as well as spanners and sockets.

All the time she sings, "The piston's connected to the little end, the little end's connected to con rod, the con rod's connected to the big end," and so on as she goes through the whole engine build. After lunch it is the cylinder head's turn to go through the engineering wizardry. Phillipa reads through her Haynes Manual and makes sure Dad makes no mistakes.

By afternoon tea it is time for a rest, so together they go for a little cycle ride at the local BMX track. They sit on the grass bank down by the river and rest.

Now that the cobwebs have been blown out, Phillipa asks, "Can I guess the emotion you talked about this morning now Dad?

Nick replies, "You've earned it, young lady. Remember the rules: five questions only and watch the eyes!"

"Yes Dad, I've thought about this all day and tried to work out a way of knowing the answer from your reaction to something I say. So remembering that Chinese chart you have on foods in the kitchen, I could say to you…" Her eyes focus with intent on his.

She begins slowly: "Fire… bitter. Love. Respect. Joy - or hate and impatience. Hmm. OK no reaction."

She tries again: "Earth. Mothering. Fairness. Worry, anxiety - sweet? OK no reaction. Metal? Uprighteousness. Courage! Sadness, depression? Contracting, seed falling. Pungent! Hmm. Still no reaction."

Then: "Water, salty. Gentleness. Conserving, gathering. Cold, fear. Fear! Got you! Your eye twinkled; you were a scaredy cat that day! What happened, Dad? Come on, tell me - what happened?" said Phillipa, with urgency.

"Yes young lady, you've been paying attention. Let's go home and have some tea, light the fire, sit down and we can go through that day, together."

Once evening has arrived and they have both eaten their preferred Saturday evening meal from the Wheat-sheaf Pub across the courtyard; washed up and put things away, Phillipa starts to pester her dad: "So when are you going to start? All day we've worked, then cleaned the tools and put them away, then cleaned and tidied up. The back door's locked and I've taken the phone off the hook. Are there any excuses you can think of now, not to get on with it Dad?"

"Well Phillipa, let me see. It could be thirsty work and it could go on for a while, especially if you keep interrupting and asking questions. Then of course, it is seven o'clock and you really need to be getting washed and ready for bed! If I'm going to recall this day, you'll need a blanket just in case you get a little cold. And if you nod off during this adventure, I'll just stop. So don't let yourself down: do the washing and changing thing and thank you for your help today."

"Well if you'd missed that tab washer or you put that crank oil seal in the wrong way round I would have lost my next

Saturday play day. So it's best someone keeps an eye on you, old man."

"They were deliberate mistakes, to make sure you were paying attention! Cheeky little imp!"

"I bet. You made a boo-boo there - I know it, you know it and that's final. Before I get changed and washed, brush my teeth and get ready and settled on the settee I want to know: is it a one-pint or a two-pint story? Just so I know how many biscuits and how much milk I'll need."

Nick shrugs his shoulders, the tea towel hanging over his shoulder as he wipes down the kitchen worktops. "You, young lady, are more and more fun to be with every day. You just get cheekier all the time. But you're still polite - that I can only admire, bless you. Now go and get changed and ready for bed and I'll nip next door and bring back my throat relaxer!"

"On my way, Chief!" little Phillipa replies and runs out of the kitchen, through the hallway, across the lounge and up the stairs to her bedroom. There she washes, brushes her teeth and gets changed into her buttercup yellow nightdress. She pulls down the corner of the duvet on her bed and throws her matching dressing gown on.

Racing down the stairs, she places the throw from her bed on to the settee and goes to the kitchen, where she reaches for a glass, fills it with milk and grabs a few savoury biscuits.

Just as she is settling down, Nick comes through the front door with two pints of Tetley's Imperial.

When Phillipa sees the two pints in her dad's hand as he walks into the lounge after locking the front door, she smiles with glee. "It really is a two-pinter, wow! I thought you just meant you would have a swifty next door and bring one home. I'll draw the curtains and put the sidelight on, and then you'd best get started before I absolutely burst. Come on Dad - I can't see your feet running in a blur across the room. Chop chop, no time to waste now."

"OK, OK, patience. Just let me sit down and settle. Pass me those coasters to put my pint glasses on would you please? Place them on the suitcase coffee table thing."

Phillipa does as she is asked and Nick puts his two pint glasses down.

"Now, young lady. Are we sitting comfortably?"

"Don't give me that, Dad! You know I'm ready, you're just stalling!"

"I was just making sure I'm sitting comfortably too, you know!"

"Yes I know, but I'm cheap labour and this is payback. I'm the organ grinder and you're the monkey, so come on, crack on!" she says with that little glint of joy in her eye as she knows she is getting near the tipping point of humour and being in trouble.

Chapter 4: Waldo's Kite

"I won't start with 'once upon a time', as you know this is not how it was. I arrived here at Murtyl's at half past eight on a summer Saturday morning. The weather was fantastic; all those trees on the green out there were heavy with leaves. The blossom had fallen and the little chestnuts were just starting to sprout. There were people walking past to get their newspapers, and walking their dogs. Cyclists were blasting down through the village on their way to Stokesley, trying to look like they were competing in the Milk Race.

"I knocked on the front door and went through it, into the house. I shouted for lady M and got silence, so I walked through the hallway and the dining room to the back door. It was open; I should have just parked my bike out the back anyway. The garage door was open and there was nobody to be seen. So I went back inside and took my riding gear off, placed my helmet on the sideboard and hung my leather jacket up. I opened my bag and put on some more relaxed clothes. I had no idea what we might be doing that day. I was just looking forward to spending the day with the wily bugger.

"Then I heard her making engine noises upstairs, and thought I'd better let her know I'm here. At the same time I was wondering if she had gone off her rocker - if you know what I mean."

Nick winks at Phillipa, who just looks at him and says, "She's just tricky Dad, really tricky!"

"So anyway she shouted down to me to wait; she would be down in a minute and then we would be off. There was no need for a flask of anything or food as we would be able to get a bite on the way. So I sat down on the big red sofa and relaxed. My shoes were off, but it didn't mean I could put my hooves up on the coffee table. I now had on my best jeans, a white, cheesecloth, loose fitting shirt and a good belt."

Phillipa interrupts: "*Cheesecloth!* What kind of fashion junky were you?"

"Young lady, if you're going to interrupt like that, then I'll stop. You can make some mental notes and ask questions later. Otherwise I can enjoy my beers in peace and you can go to bed."

Phillipa answers, in dismay, "Message understood."

He carries on, a glint of fun in his eyes. "So as I was saying, I was dressed in what I thought to be 'looking quite cool' gear, as Lady M floated down the stairs. She had her hair up, in a style I hadn't seen before. There was a little bit of red lippy on, and an off-white fitted blouse and some hipster jeans, which were not too tight, with a little flare at the bottom. She was wearing brown Dealer Boots that were polished and she carried a navy blue polo neck jumper over her arm.

"Murtyl asked if I was set for the day and did I have a strong stomach as well as a warm jumper and maybe a jacket. I replied, "Yes ma'am, I have both – if it is OK to use my bike jacket!" Then we were off.

"I said, "Where to, Murtyl?"

"Bagby," she replied. "The weather is looking good and I have some friends to catch up with."

"Where is Bagby?"

"Thirkelby, lad!"

"OK, where is Thirkelby?"

"It is on the old A19, a little after Thirsk on the way to York. You must have ridden through it many a time. Don't you pay any attention? Or is it just flat out and enjoy the road and not the scenery?"

"I replied, "I know where you mean now. Isn't there a stud farm just there?"

"Yes there is Nick, so you do pay a little attention. You may just need to be on the ball today. Once I have the Ice Blue girl out of the garage, you can lock up, get in and we can go. We need to move as there a schedule to keep to just now!" I replied that I was on it and we were off.

"The little old Ice Blue Healey ran beautifully, as ever. I had the privilege of driving, while Lady M made those weird noises again. She was moving her hands and head in the most peculiar way. I couldn't ask what she was doing, as the wind buffeted around us. As we went down the A19 heading south, she was just away in her own world. I took the Thirsk, York turn-off on the new A 19 and headed to York. While waiting to get past a truck, I caught her attention and was able to get that question in.

"Oh just taking myself through a sequence as I need to remind myself of some intricate moves for later!'

"As ever, I was none the wiser, young lady. So after about fifteen minutes we were pulling up at the smallest airstrip I had ever seen. I brought the car to rest in a cloud of dust and Murtyl was in the clubhouse and out in just a few moments, keys in her hand and shouting, "Come on, lad!" So I ran and caught her up.

"We stopped running by a little Cessna 150 single engined propeller driven aeroplane. She unlocked the door and told me to get in the port seat, which to you and me is the left, as you would if you were being taught to fly. She then went and stuck a piece of metal into some drain points on each wing and examined it. I later found out this was to check for water in the fuel. Then she looked over the propeller and the wings; checked that the elevators and rudder moved

81

smoothly - and the ailerons too! Finally she checked the oil level in the Rolls-Royce 4-cylinder engine, dropped its cover back down and clipped all the safety latches down. It all took her about four minutes.

"She got in the aeroplane, placed a map on my knee and said, "Netherthorpe. Find it and where we are now. There's 8/8 visibility and next to zero wind, so dead reckoning will be easy. PPR already requested; we just need to start up, check each magneto is effective, power check, then call in for clearance and go." She taxied forward a little, called into the tower for clearance, and then we were off, heading down the hill towards the old A19 and into next to no breeze. The runway could only have been two hundred and fifty yards long and I did not think there was enough room.

"I wanted to know where we were off to; she just gave me an 'are you stupid?' look. I then realised that Netherthorpe must be where we were heading. We were in the air in less than two hundred yards and climbing with ten percent flaps. It was the first time in a light aircraft for me so I was a little dumbstruck. Around one hundred feet the flaps were taken off and the little aircraft surged forward - almost like the handbrake had been take off. They call that drag, you know.

"Now at four thousand feet, we levelled off and she started to explain the instruments. That was not too hard to follow. She then asked me to hold the yoke and place my feet on the rudder pedals. I did this, but was sweating a bit! We were heading pretty much due south and she pointed out the power stations that were visible: Drax and a few others which pretty much made it a straight line all the way to the River Trent. I was asked to follow the controls as she moved them: left rudder and the aeroplane yawed to the left, a bit like sliding and skidding. The wings gave less lift and so we lost a little height. Rudder off and a little bit of throttle and she climbed. Throttle back a little and she flew straight and level again. The yoke turned to the right and the aeroplane tilted; once tilted the yoke input was taken off but the aeroplane lost height again, slipping sideways. Left rudder was applied and height was maintained. This was fun! All the time Murtyl was calm, smiling and relaxed.

"We climbed to maybe eight thousand feet; she looked around and heaved the yoke back. The aeroplane climbed violently then slowed. A squealer started and Murtyl just held the stick back until it stalled. The bugger then let all the controls go and looked at me. She smiled and folded her arms. The nose dropped, the tail flipped up behind us and we were falling! The aeroplane started to rotate clockwise. I instinctively pushed the yoke fully forward with full left rudder - why the left rudder I will never know but it seemed to be the right thing to do. Next thing I know we are at four thousand feet and I'm looking at her to try and figure out what to do next. The engine tone had changed, as if the propeller was gripping the air again. I started to ease back on the stick and the nose came up. We were straight and level again in no time. She said I was doing well and we practised it a few more times. Then she looked at her little Rolex on the inside of her left wrist and said it was time to press on. The Cessna was trimmed out and we cruised the rest of the way at about one hundred and five knots."

Nick takes a slurp of his beer and little Pip's hand shoots up: "Dad that's not all that happened that day – you've only taken one slurp. You've gone a little white and a bit sweaty - is that when you were frightened?"

Nick replies, "Sweetheart, that was just the beginning of the day, and I've cut that short so you're not up too late!"

"Fantastic, I was getting worried Murtyl was going to let me down!"

"I don't think she ever let anybody down, it was just not in her nature. Being the best of the best in every way was not just a habit, but I think a rule!"

Nick carries on with his story: "So I looked down from four thousand feet and could not make out the little airstrip. Murtyl adjusted the frequency on the wireless, then called into her microphone, "Netherthorpe Radio, Golf, Alpha, Whiskey, Lima, Alpha, inbound, request airfield information."

They came back with, "Netherthorpe Tower to Golf, Lima, Alpha, circuit clear, wind west knots, use runway zero nine, approach at will. Good to hear your voice."

"She replied, "Good to hear yours, Ducky; will call finals!" She pointed out on the map exactly where we were, and flew directly over the centre of the runway at two thousand feet, always looking right and left for any other aircraft. She also pointed out a few local landmarks including a smoking chimney, which she called the glass factory and the chicken sheds of a poultry farm. These were the local spots to look for, as there were no hills, I could see!

"As we started our descent, I followed her instructions, checking my belt was tight and the door was closed on our downwind leg. She did the same, and then pulled out the 'Carburettor Heat' knob. When I asked what that was for, I was told that during descent, icing of the carburettor could mean complete engine failure. This could be seen as dangerous and viewed as not too sporting!

"About three hundred yards out Murtyl turned again in line with the runway and called to the Tower, "Golf, Lima, Alpha

– finals," which I think meant committed, and pulled back on the throttle. The little aeroplane slowed and started to lose height. At around a thousand feet she gave the little aircraft some flap - ten, twenty, then thirty degrees - and dropped her nose by pushing the yoke forward. She put a little throttle back on to maintain some of the height and, once we were over the road and a wire fence, she asked where I thought we should be on the runway. I pointed to the markers at the beginning of the two hundred and fifty yard runway. She shook her head, pointing to a location much closer to the clubhouse: "Why taxi when you can fly?'

"We flew a little further at maybe one hundred feet then the power came off and my stomach came up through my throat. We dropped like a stone, then she pulled back on the yoke and my tummy went out through me arse, sorry backside. My eyes were tightly closed and before I knew it, we were taxiing to the parking area. I never even felt us make contact with the ground."

Nick takes another slurp while Pip drinks a little milk. They wipe their mouths in unison and Nick carries on.

"She shut the engine down after checking the oil pressure and so on were correct in idle, then jumped out and placed some chocks under the wheel: "Come on lad, you can meet a few friends of mine and have some lunch."

"I did not think I was up to much lunch but forced down a bit of chicken pie and a Coca Cola. During this time I was introduced to 'Ducky' who was actually the Chief Flying Instructor, Ian Drake and a few other people. Seemingly we were all off to a 'fly in'. This meant we would all fly in different aeroplanes to a field that had once been used during World War II by an active squadron. The farmer who farmed this land during World War II would allow them to do this once a year, as a mark of respect to the brave men from back then. There would have been about fifteen little aircraft; then a few others from different airfields turned up. They all talked flying and remembered those brave men and said a prayer.

"Just as I thought it was all over, a red and white biplane turned up and landed. This plane was pretty spectacular. Its call sign, or registration number, was G-WILD and the letters all fitted onto the tail fin – it would normally be down the side of the fuselage, but on the side of the fuselage was written TOYOTA.

"They all shouted, "Four Eyes has made it!" and cheered. The plane taxied up and a few people looked at each other and then at me. My knees started to wobble a bit, but I knew not why!

"A little fellow called Waldo jumped out of the Pitts Special and walked over to Murtyl. He shouted at her, "You've got twenty minutes, then I need to be away for a show. She's full of fuel and a little heavy. Put her through her paces; I'm not usually on the ground to watch! No smoke though!"

"At this we were off. I was pushed into the front seat and told to strap in hard - it was a five-point blinking harness! I had no time to think! She was in the back seat in a flash. I had never seen that look of wild concentration on her face before; I think she was excited to be free at a stick again. I grabbed the leather-flying helmet she lobbed over from her seat to me and put it on. There was a tap on my right shoulder with a communications, or 'comms' lead showing in her hand.

"She shouted, "Plug yours in then I can talk to you!" Then the great big motor turned and roared into life – boy, it was loud! The propeller was massive and as it spun, the air it pushed over us was fierce. The little windscreen deflected it a bit but not that much. As we taxied round, then towards the other end of the field, she kept pointing the nose from side to side. I ask why, and she told me through my headset the she had no view of anything in front and by moving the aeroplane from side to side, she could see ahead. Anyway we got to the end of the field; she turned the thing around and shouted, "Arms folded, touch nothing and don't throw up in Waldo's kite!'

"It dawned on me slowly, as the engine roared and the propeller thrashed against the air, creating thrust, what she had been doing in the car, the crazy lady. Due to the wash from the propeller, she let the brakes off with the tail already in the air. The aeroplane thundered, bursting forward, its acceleration greater and greater. I was thrust further and further back into the seat. I tightened my harness even tighter and started to pray: please let me live! This was the first time it had ever crossed my mind that Murtyl might be as mad as a hatter.

"Then, through my earphones, I heard that little 'Muttley' snigger and Murtyl muttered something like, "Going up." I saw the stick ease and then strike back rather firmly; the throttle remained where it was. We were vertical! Still accelerating, blinking heck we were still accelerating Pip! The stick was in the neutral or centre position, then it flicked wildly to the right. She started to spin, or rotate or whatever they say. Not like a fairground ride - it spun like a spinning top. I didn't know where the hell I was! As the Pitts Special started to slow on the vertical, Murtyl stopped the rotation. The prop screamed as it tore at the air for grip; the throttle was closed and we started to fall backwards; we were still pointing up but we were going backwards. The right rudder slammed against the bulkhead and the left rose up and caught my flailing shin. Damn, that hurt. The nose of the Pitts seemed to fall faster and rotated around the tail. We were heading straight towards the damn ground now.

"Then the throttle went fully home, the motor roared from idle to flat out and the prop disappeared in front of my eyes again. With gravity helping us, the acceleration was just crazy. My eyes were still heading towards the back of my head as they had done on the way up. I don't really know but at about five hundred feet, the stick came back - hard back; my stomach tried physically to get out of my bottom. My head was pushed in so I looked like a tortoise. She never told me to hold my breath during a manoeuvre but I soon learned to brace myself rigid as soon as I saw the stick or a pedal twitch by an eighth of an inch. We climbed to about one thousand feet, and again there was input; it was so quick I nearly missed it and nearly lost my head as the beast rotated in a forty-five degree roll. Three seconds later, another forty-five degree roll. The pedals and stick movement were tiny, and almost a blur to me now. Another quarter roll, then another - now we were upside down. Upside down, two hundred miles per hour. I just wanted to live Pip, I just wanted to live!

"We started to climb. We were still upside down, so when the stick went forward I thought we were going to dive but no, we went up. The input stayed there; slight alterations were made to the stick and rudder but we were doing an outside blinking loop. At the top we flipped right way up, started gently towards the ground and then barrel rolled twice. I knew not where we were; I did know I did not like it.

"She peeled round gently and flew towards a main road. We flipped upside down about three hundred feet above a big road sign and were off again. I was in a bit of a daze and next thing I knew we were landing back in the same field. We taxied in with the same side-to-side movement and Murtyl asked me if I had enjoyed the little joy ride!"

"I answered, "I never want to fly again.""

"Murtyl just laughed and replied, "I will teach you when you're ready; you'll love it!"

"Dad, dad, that can't be it, you're nearly through your two sherbets. While I go to the bathroom, you could nip next door and bring another home. You can also tell me what they say when they see your face, 'cos you look like a ghost!" says Pip.

"I think I may just do that. If I don't finish this episode I won't sleep tonight and that just will not do! So run upstairs and do what you have to, I'll be back in five minutes, Sweetheart."

Pip jumps up and runs straight to the bathroom with her arms spread out, making aeroplane noises.

Nick comes back into the house with his third pint and locks the front door behind him. In the lounge, Pip is already settled back into her listening position, blanket wrapped over her little legs.

When she sees him with the lights of the room turned on, she bursts out laughing.

"You look all shaken up Dad! Your skin is a bluey white and you look like you've shrunk! What did the lads say in the pub when they saw you?"

"Well Pip, I have to say I got a few looks and I was asked if I had just been in a car crash, a fight or got out of jail or something. I tried to explain I was telling you a story of a time with an old friend. Now they want to hear it all. So I told them: they could be pretty sure that you would let them all know in good time!"

"Great, I'll get a few Cokes out of that then!" she says with a cunning smile and that glint in her eyes. "Come on then Dad, park it and crack on, I want it finished before you chase me off to bed."

Nick answers with a worn-out smile. "Your wish is my command, but you have to give me a minute to settle and stop shaking. I still have nightmares about heading straight into the turf at two hundred miles an hour!"

"Oh come on Dad, you know she was better than that!"

"Yes I did, but after eventually clawing my backside out of that Pitts Special, my legs were pretty wobbly. I went down on my knees and kissed the ground! As I looked up, all the people there were laughing and congratulating Murtyl on an excellent display routine. My mind started to understand what she had been doing in the car with her hands and head movements. I was just about to get up and have my first ever stern word with her, when out of the corner of my eye I saw some pretty thick foliage sticking out of the undercarriage.

Everything went black then; I must have fainted.

"I woke up in the recovery position with sick all over me. Murtyl was apologising for not warning me about what she had arranged and done, but she thought I was made of sterner stuff and I had to pull myself together; we needed to fly back to Bagby and then go home. She would debrief me there. Debrief me! I was not in the air force or the blinking army; I just did not understand. Before I got myself fully together, I received many pats on the back, and 'good to meet you, we've heard so much about you'- all that malarkey.

"Then, we were up in the blasted air again. I was not touching anything. I just kept mumbling, "Straight and level, straight and level please." We arrived back at Bagby an hour or so later and she drove us back here. I was still ill; I had not recovered and still felt wibbly-wobbly. Murtyl sorted some soup out and apologised to me again. I started to feel a bit better and she told me it would not be safe for me to ride home that evening, then started to ply me with brandy. Gosh, I hate that stuff, but right enough I came round and started to ask the correct questions!

"I know, I know what those questions are, Dad," says Pip.

"Yes I know you do, but pop them out just in case you're slacking!"

"Who, what, where, why and when - but not necessarily in that order. Yes?"

Nick answers, "Ye-es. I'll give you that one."

Pip comes back with, "Ye-es, and if you don't get back on track you'll be after a fourth sherbet before you get started again. I can't stay up all night waiting for you to get started. So stop standing, sit and crack on will you!" She pauses just long enough for Nick to start to answer her and adds that blessed word: "Please?"

Nick sits down, looks at his daughter as if shocked and says, "You are a cheeky little sod." Pip just smiles at her dad, knowing he loves her with all his heart. She waves her hand elegantly towards the sofa he has been sitting on and winks at him. He does as she instructed and carries on with his story.

"So I had had a few brandies with Murtyl and started to ask the five questions, beginning with, "When did you learn to fly like that?" Murtyl told me that Robert Benoist, the great World War I fighter ace, had taught her most of the individual moves before World War II, when she was a girl. You'll remember that great man from her first diary." Nick looks at Pip and she nods enthusiastically.

"Murtyl then went on to say that she knew all the airfields from her second job during World War II, which was delivering military aircraft to the front lines as it were. She kept in touch with a few people who went to the Remembrance Ceremony fly-ins and had met Waldo, the pilot with the Pitts Special. She had recognised the aircraft from the opening credits on *Grandstand* or *World of Sport* - which were the Saturday afternoon sports television programmes, back in the dark ages. She had seen his eyes rolling in and out of their sockets and had wanted to know how much G-force this specially built aerobatic aeroplane could pull.

"Waldo was World Aerobatics Champion at the time and she bloody well challenged him to a duel in the air - not shooting at each other, but a fly-off. I'm telling you Pip, she was nuts. Anyway, Waldo checked her out and old Ducky had verified she was safe to fly. Waldo trusted Ducky as he had taught him to fly at Netherthorpe and so it was on! God almighty, they were at it! He took her up and went through his routine; she then mirrored it! They were at it seemingly for five or more hours, except for coming down for fuel and nature breaks. In the end they shook hands. She said he was brilliant but had a habit of just not reversing long enough at the top of his stall, and he said if a man can ever please her he would like to meet him. She was as good as he had ever encountered and she could have his ride any time! This just happened to be the any time; I got the 'show and tell' routine and nearly pooped my pants!"

"Murtyl explained that when racing a bike, a car or flying an aircraft, practising the precise movements and living the moment allowed the instinct or "speeditus", being inspiration, to flow. It allowed for expected things to be felt and not thought about. Then if something went wrong, you had much more time to make the correct, save-a-life decision. I suppose when I think about it, that is how she approached everything, Discipline, planning, knowledge and nothing left to chance. It meant she could cope with the unexpected and react in the manner she did. God I loved that woman!"

"It was only in the morning, when I looked in the mirror with a very stiff neck, that I saw the result of the previous day's flying. My temples were bruised; the side of my head was bruise; my eyes were darker than normal and there was a cut on the bridge of my great big ruddy nose!"

Pip butts in with, "Yes it is, Dad!" and Nick throws a coaster at her with enthusiasm, answering with, "Do you want to hear the end of this?"

She replies, "I think I better had; who knows where it will take us?" and Nick opens his eyes wide and looks at his daughter, not knowing what to answer her with.

He carries on. "The backs of both of my hands were battered and I had a loose tooth. Then slowly it dawned on me: nobody had mentioned my state because I think I looked so ill. I must have passed out part of the way through Madam's blinking display and flailed around the cockpit like a rag doll with a seat belt on. At the time I could not understand why my washed out jeans were really dark around the crotch, but when I think about it…"

Pip bursts out laughing, creasing herself up as her sides start to ache at the thought of her Dad being so frightened he'd passed out, wet himself and beaten himself up.

"It's not funny young lady; I hope nobody ever scares you that way, and if they do you'd better have your Tena Lady pants on!"

Pip retorts with, "You mean nappies. Nobody could scare me that much, not even herself, the trickiest of tricksters."

"Well Sweetheart, I had black and blue arms and legs; my head was a mess and I took a few days to recover. I have never been in an aerobatic aeroplane since, and nor will I! I will tan your backside if you tell the guys in the pub that part. It was between Murtyl and me - even your mum knew not what you know now. So pull yourself together, wipe the tears from your eyes and get to bed!"

He stands up to take his glass through to the kitchen. He wobbles and sits down again, looks at Pip and says, "Get on with you. I just need a minute to get over that day again. Go on now, go!"

Pip runs upstairs and wriggles into her bed, knowing it is way past her bed time, worrying about the scaredy cat downstairs and wondering how on earth she will get to sleep with that day vivid in her mind. How can she keep her mouth shut with Dad's friends in the pub? Will they get that engine done on time?

So much to think about and so much sleeping to do!

Chapter 5: The Package

"Now young lady, off to sleep with you and you can ask questions while we finish with that cylinder head in the morning. OK?"

"Yes Dad, give me a hug and know I love you and I'm away!"

Nick replied, "I love you too!"

"As much as Lady M?"

"A whole lot more my little angel, now sleep!" he replied.

"See you in the morning." Phillipa called as her bedroom door closed and her light went out.

Downstairs, Nick sat on the sofa and smiled. It was a long time since he had thought through that day of terror. Looking back on it now it didn't seem so bad. Maybe he should take Pip to the little airfields and show her round. Maybe, if she asked - yes that was a nice idea. She deserved a day out just for her. A little flight too with Ducky, if he still remembered 'he who could chunder!'

Nick fell asleep on the sofa; his three beers and the excitement had taken its toll. The next thing he knew he was being addressed sternly, a finger poking him in the shoulder and a little angel, in her nightie, with a glass of milk in one hand telling him to get to bed; that she did not need spying on in the middle of the night when she had the 'munchies'. By the time Nick came round enough to realise what was going on, the little angel had gone. He stretched and heaved himself up. Then made his way to his own bed for some proper sleep.

Sunday they were back in the garage again running the same routine but with the cylinder head. Pip asked questions about flying: could he fly? Could she fly? When?

Nick concentrated on the valve lapping and tried to explain: Murtyl had taught him to fly but he had no licence. It was an expensive activity, but... well of course. A little later in the summer he would take her to show her the two little airfields and see if any of the people there still remembered him. Maybe - just maybe – (but no promises) he could get her a ride; but not an aerobatic one!

They built the cylinder head up and torqued it down on to the cylinder block. Placed the pushrods in and put the camshaft rocker in place. Tightened it down and set the valve gaps several times just to be sure.

They fitted the distributor and set the timing then attached the high-tension leads in the correct firing order: 1-3-4-2. Filled a new oil filter with oil, married it to the engine, and filled the engine up with oil. It was ready to go, and they were on time. The engine could be picked up that night when Pip was in bed; the team would fit it during their spare time and call when the car was ready to start. Pip would be invited to do the honours of being the starter person. That was the plan!

Two days later, Nick was about to bundle Pip off to school on the school bus and she saw the postman. "Dad, it's today, today I tell you. I can see in Postie's eyes he has a different kind of parcel. I can feel it. Have you heard from Ron?"

"No little lady, I have not and how could you know from the Postie at fifty yards?" Nick replied.

"It is, Dad, it is. You had that buzzing in your ear. I feel it in my bones; it's like magic. Only Mum or Murtyl could stir that much up for us both to feel!"

The postman came closer and Pip held her father's hand tighter and tighter. The postman reached into his bag and pulled out a big, brown, deep, rectangular package: "Sign, please Nick - just here, that's right. The whole village knows this is what you have been hoping for. Make her proud lad, make her proud!"

Pip piped up, "Don't worry - I'll keep an eye on him and double check everything!"

Nick turned and drifted towards the little cottage, dragging Pip with him. Pip shouted at her dad, "Yippeeee! No school today."

Nick suddenly came out of his trance and put his responsible head on. "Sorry Pip, you have to go. I know you are excited, just as I am. I have a full day planned so how about we make a deal? I do not open the package, diary or not, until you are home here with me. We do it together. Deal?"

Pip raised her right hand and went through all those disgusting actions, and said, "Done." Then off she went to school, having full trust in her father's integrity.

Chapter 6: Beetle

Roscoe H. Hillenkoetter was director of Central Intelligence for the Central Intelligence Agency in the United States from 1947 to 1950. He was an ex-navy man who looked at intelligence and overviewed things for his superior, Harry S. Truman, the President. He knew of the case but had seen different departments come in with reports and he had not put them together to see the bigger picture, as it were. He was heading for retirement and was not really looking to get the dog's tail wagging too much before he got to that well-earned rest duty starting on October 7th, 1950

His successor, the man who would take over, was General Walter Bedell Smith, a former US Army boy. In 1943, he ran the

Allied Invasion Campaign into Italy. He later became Eisenhower's Chief of Staff at the Supreme Headquarters Allied Expeditionary Force (SHAEF). Walter Smith acquired a reputation for representing Eisenhower as a diplomat in sensitive areas such as the negotiations of the Nazi surrender, late during World War II. At the same time he was decisive and was known as Eisenhower's hatchet man!

He had started as a private in the army and had worked his way up from the bottom, eventually becoming the United States Ambassador to the Soviet Union from April 3rd, 1946 to Christmas Day, 1948. He was a short back and sides man with slicked back hair. The bottom lip protruded slightly ahead of the upper and his eyes were close together. His military style, with back bolt upright and his precision pressed uniform, took no mercy on the unwary casual approach.

When he took office with the CIA he was accountable directly to Eisenhower and Franklin D. Roosevelt. The US Security Services had lost their direction and punch during the war and post-war years. Walter Bedell 'Beetle' Smith was going to change that. He gave the CIA a whole new place in the world. He redefined and reorganised the CIA in structure and purpose. The CIA became in the first instance responsible for covert operations outside the USA.

He may have been planning this when taking the position but it became apparent to him when a number of files crossed his desk after a mishap. As part of a new broom sweeping through and looking for dead wood, as it were, to go, a number of staff members were under pressure to show willing. Two guys, from two different departments, walked into each other while each were moving files. They apologised to each other and started to sort the files out as they picked them up off the floor. Beetle just happened to be there at the wrong time and observed the farce. He demanded that all the files went to his office and started to wade through them. What caught his eye was that two separate departments within the CIA were chasing the same thing from different angles. Both had lost their way; both had lost the ability to investigate deeply. They were obviously flabby and lacking the spirit he required, physically or by stealth.

He brought in two of his own preferred men from outside the agency, then set them off like rats in a maze. He chose the first because he was a paperwork demon, wore glasses and looked a little like Clark Kent - just a little narrower at the shoulders and wider at the hips. The counterpart was the opposite. Yes, he was ex-army but he was also a former Chicago hitman who rose in the army during World War II and was spotted by his now boss's trusted elite. He was quick and decisive, ruthless and hid his shifty eyes under his wide-brimmed felt hat. The fact that he wore a suit meant nothing; it just hid his athleticism and potential speed. Beetle took their files and studied them.

They were both on the same case; they sent reports in weekly to Beetle of their progress and met up with him individually on a monthly basis. The monthly meetings were face to face at variable times in his office; not even Beetle's secretary knew the full details of what was going on. The search the two men were engaged in was to confirm a hunch that Beetle was hoping would be found to be incorrect. Sadly, Beetle knew how often his hunches were off the firing range, and how often they struck the bull's-eye.

This hunch was making him sweat and kept him up most nights. Could it be possible that the organisation buying up oil fields was aligned to the people who seemed to be hovering around top-secret nuclear test sites and potential installations? The dates matched and that was about all he had to go on but his rats were on the run now! All he could do was wait then compile his report and go to Eik and Roosevelt with his assumptions, fears, and agents' findings

His next dilemma was: should he use his contacts in the Soviet Union from his ambassador days - the Canadians from the 1945 Rheims Negotiations in France for the German surrender? He could also talk to the UK, the French and the Australians and so on. He knew about the up and coming Anglo/Australian nuclear tests to come and wanted to know if any of their men had similar fears. He needed a Go Button!

With no concrete evidence and no defined target he had nothing. Resources only just allowed him to use the two guys he was using. This reorganisation was taking its toll on him and his trusted staff. There were fifty two states acting like fifty two independent countries; to bring them under one intelligence net was proving to be a completely new kind of battle. Getting rid of bad personnel was easy, the decision and the action of moving them out no problem. However, training and recruiting new personnel with the appropriate skills was a whole different ball game. Training new personnel, even ex-military, was going to take time.

The only question Beetle had was: was there really an enemy out there? If there was, would it be the CIA's responsibility to find that enemy, if it was outside the USA? Then even if it *was* outside, could it be a threat to the USA?

He waited for the reports to arrive with the agents at the allotted time. Neither had known each other before, so cross-referencing should not happen. They were from different backgrounds: one university and the other the Mafia. Their modus operandi was to work from two divergent directions. They would meet for the first time in his office, with their reports for him to go through, question and assess at 0600 hrs.

Beetle waited. 0600 hrs came and went. He made his own coffee and went back to his desk, going through the files to hand, knowing his secure secretaries would be in at 0830 hrs. The big hand swung slowly past the thirty-five minute mark and his feet began to tap the floor beneath his leather inlaid teak desk. His chair rocked back and forth, just a little but enough to creak and let him know he was beginning to worry. For God's sake! They were coming from different parts of the States. They could not both be late for the same appointment at the same time in the same bloody office. They were both ex-military and knew punctuality and discipline were key to the modern way.

0710 hrs. Where the hell were they? Eventually he made the decision to call his superiors. They both wanted a meeting and a report; they both received blank sheets with a separate little note saying, "Men down. Meet 3 in 1 white." It meant he had lost men; he required the three of them to meet urgently and with Roosevelt's health the way it was, the White House would be the quickest and safest place.

The meeting took place in the Oval Office that evening at 2046 hrs. It lasted seven minutes. Beetle came out knowing he had a whole new world to try and cover.

The CIA was not equipped, staffed or trained for this kind of work. His budget was now almost limitless after the meeting just a few minutes before. He was going to have to recruit the best; but who would assess them? He needed men on the ground - same problem! Then he needed coordinators to pool and assess the information. Up all night, he worked until his secretary came in to a deluge of instructions. As she struggled out of his office with her work, he started working out ways to get in contact with organisations abroad. By the time it was lunch for most people, he was in the air on the way to Europe to set up a meeting with any counterparts he could. He just hoped his stomach was wrong and his hunch was crazy. The only two people he had spoken to had probably bought it. He just hoped his fears were wrong, inasmuch as his two men were not dead.

Chapter 7: Bella

Beetle did not know, however, that his two men had met each other not two weeks earlier. They had both woken in a darkened room; neither had clothes, neither was completely compos mentis and both were suffering the after-effects of the drugs that had been administered. The darkened room was deep underground; the walls of the room were dry and cool. There were no openings to be found, just as there were no creature comforts. The first of them groaned and started to explore his surrounding with his hand, slowly feeling across the floor and trying to understand where he was. Touching another naked body was an added shock; there was another person in the room. The second agent started to come round. Both had splitting headaches, bruises and pains. They started to converse warily: who was who - and why were they both in this cell, if it was a cell of some sort? The first agent – a big guy - was slightly ahead of the other in his recovery from the sedatives they had been given. He heard only the voice of the second agent as he ran his hands over a face and shoulders in the dark. They were nameless to each other, but the smaller guy – later known as the Bookworm - began to recognise the Chicago hood's gravelly tones. They began to search around the cell with their bare hands, starting in opposite directions, reporting to each other their findings. Other than spiders' webs and dust, nothing was felt or found until they both came across a smooth, steel door with no handles. Desperately parched with thirst, they each sank to the floor and leaned with their backs to a wall.

No water and blind in the dark, they started to talk. Neither had an idea of where they were but they did start to discuss the cases they had been following when, for both of them, the world had turned to darkness. The pieces did not fit but being in this cell meant they were onto something - they just could not put the parts of the puzzle together.

A while later, the door opened and a blinding white light flooded the room. Both froze, not knowing what to expect. The big man had been trained but not for this, in peace time! He was the first to be taken out of the cell. The Bookworm left; the door slammed shut and there was still no water. He started to sweat with fear, desperately trying to figure where he was and what was going on.

The big man was marched forward with a wire loop around his neck, cutting deep into his throat. One end of the cheese wire was attached to a steel tube and the other end was threaded through the tube. His handler held the four foot long tube in one hand; the end of this cheese wire was linked to a simple wooden handle in the other hand. The handler was behind the unclothed agent, who was being marched forward through a corridor that appeared hand-carved out of the rock. The floor had been levelled with concrete but the walls were hewn out of some natural stone and he was buggered if he had seen anything like it before. Everywhere was well lit; the wiring was neatly capped into the upper part of the walls. Even if the neck contraption had not been attached to him, they were too high to jump at. A second handler led the way; it seemed to be miles they walked, but in reality it was about four hundred yards - twice around the complex but enough to keep the agent completely disorientated.

The second handler was armed and militarily neat and tidy but the uniform was, if anything, theatrical: bigger and louder than need be. No camouflage was required in this place. His weapon was a Colt 0.45 Pistol; not quick to draw but a damned good stopper if you got in the way of its exhaust projectile. Accurate over a short distance, it did not look used. The big guy surmised that security was a priority but not a worry, otherwise training and wear marks would have shown on the pistol. Then again this place could be new. Where the hell were they?

They stopped. To his right, a door opened and he was guided in. He saw in front of him a dental chair with arm, leg and head straps. He was physically directed into the chair and strapped down. The choking neck wire was not removed from his burning neck until he was secured with one-and-a-half inch wide leather straps that were buckled down so tightly he winced in pain. He could taste and smell in the air that this room had been cleaned and disinfected since it had last been used. The lighting was uncomfortably bright and the heat that radiated from these lights was oppressively hot. He could not move and just stared at the ceiling hewn from the rock and waited for the next thing to happen. He was as good as dead and could only hope this was some kind of CIA and Beetle test. The room he was in was actually only five feet from his cellmate - he had been walked around for long enough to completely disorientate him.

A small lady glided into the room. The big guy was, as before, defenceless. He could just see her out of the corner of his eye. She introduced herself as Ciao Bella and asked the guards to leave, as she needed them not now.

Walking around her prey, she looked over her equipment: sodium pentothal and wires which were connected to electrodes leading to various recording devices. He was thinking he could cope with this. She turned to toward him, angelic and beautiful. Then she winked and smiled a knowing smile, as she twirled a sharpened pencil in her fingers.

His mind raced: when was the questioner going to come into the room? What was in store for him and when the hell would it start?

Ciao Bella connected wires to his fingertips on either hand, then electrodes above and below his heart. She switched a machine on and looked at him. Her smooth lips parted slowly as she looked down at his penis, her tongue protruding slightly in a seductive way. The top three buttons were undone on her tight, white blouse and his mind started to burn in confusion; his desire started to show. At that, she gently leaned forward, placing her left hand on his upper thigh and looking at him with sexy 'I want you' eyes. His eyes flickered from her blue-grey orbs to her cleavage and back.

Excitement and the fear of letting the side down burned into his soul. No one had ever suggested there was a test like this. Then her right hand came down gently and slowly toward his outer right thigh and started to stroke slowly up the leg. As it reached the mid area, it started to move over the centre towards the inner thigh, then on, towards his genitals. He could do nothing but look with frustration down her blouse, and his excitement began throb. She smiled, then with one sudden movement thrust the sharpened pencil deep into his groin, just above the artery. Unable to move, he screamed in shock and pain. She snapped the end of the protruding pencil off and pushed what was left into his leg, deeper into his muscle, her thumb flicking the jagged end of the pencil under his skin. As the muscle relaxed it would move just a thousandth of an inch or so, causing the nerves to fire again, the muscle to tense and pain to surge through his central nervous system once more.

She moved back slowly, smiling and said, "A lover's touch for my darling!" then bent forward again and kissed him on the lips. He had bitten down so hard that he could feel shattered bits of teeth in his mouth. These were from three molars - two from the bottom right and one from the upper left - plus one incisor also from the upper left and an amount of tongue he could not imagine.

Daintily Ciao Bella turned and walked away, staying just within his field of vision, and ran a tap, rinsing, emptying and filling a glass vessel with water. She returned and held the vessel above his mouth. She offered the water to him and he blinked to say 'please', opening his mouth. He was desperate for the cool liquid to flow over his parched and sore mouth and tongue. The water entered his mouth in a controlled easy flow, but it was ice-cold and the now unprotected nerves sent sensations of agony screaming to his brain. The water he so eagerly required was evacuated at speed. Ciao Bella shook her head, then place her left forefinger to her lips as if to say 'Shhh my darling' and poured the rest of the ice-cold water over his testicles. The sweat from his body was excreted with enthusiasm as he felt his bladder and bowels give way.

She left the room, knowing his muscles would twitch and the pencil would work its way deeper and deeper into the flesh, creating more and more pain. The blood would congeal in a while, giving her time to have lunch, coffee and a well-earned cigarette.

She returned forty-five minutes later, knowing the Bookworm would have heard the gangster's pain; he would be cracking under the mental strain. All she needed to do with this one now was have a little chat, along the lines of "Would you mind telling me what I would like to know? I have studied under the best and have lots of the latest equipment: water boarding, toe nails, electric convulsion and shock. All the most up to date drugs are to hand, but I myself do prefer the personal touch, don't you?"

The gangster peered through his crying eyes in utter amazement. His mind was spinning, screaming in terror from this little blond lady. "What the hell can she do now? I just want to die!" ran through his mind.

Delicately, Ciao Bella picked up a cheese grater, held the flat of her left hand on his breast and firmly drew the skin down towards his navel, pulling the skin tight. Her right hand with the grater was scraped across his skin, cutting and scratching. The blood started to flow profusely from the tortured dermis. She smiled again, staring lovingly into his eyes. Then she bent down to the floor, and picked something up. His imagination was now running out of control. None of this was in any manual; there was no way he could withstand the pain. His only hope was to exhale and hold on until he passed out - knowing that when he came round, she would be there with other bastard tricks.

He desperately searched his tooth for his cyanide pill but that was gone; what was left of his tongue found only the sharp edges of shattered teeth. She stood upright, her blouse a little further undone, the cheese grater still in her right hand. She held her left hand above his wounded, burning chest and delicately sprinkled salt all over him. It all burned again with agonising ferocity. Even without water entering his system, God only knows how much sweat leaped forth from his drenched pores.

He answered her questions and then gave up, hoping to be allowed to die, with less pain.

It was the Bookworm's turn the next day. The gangster had told him of the horrors of the treatment and the seductive lady's beguiling beauty. His instruction was just to talk; talk and let it all out. Whatever you know, tell her! In fricking reality, neither of us know bloody anything!

A few days later, the two agents were taken to sea on the Ghana run. Their wounds were becoming infected so they had been given food and water to help keep their strength up. Maybe there was a little hope: they were taken onto the deck of the vessel and it was the first daylight either had seen since they could remember. The Mediterranean sun burned down on them both. Their eyes smarted with pain, as did their skin. The soles of their feet screamed and blistered with the heat of the deck on-board the ship. They leant against the railings, still with no clothes. Both were too weak to try an escape. They looked around; they were able to see and recognise that the ship was an American built Liberty class vessel with the accommodation and engine room midships. A troop of maybe sixteen coloured guys were also brought on deck. These guys were placed next to them; all lined up with nowhere to go. Chum was thrown over the side of the vessel, which had been hove to. There were no other vessels to be seen from this, the port side. Two deckhands undid some shackles and the railings, hinged at the bottom, rotated around the hinges and disappeared over the side of the vessel.

Ciao Bella stood there in her skirt and blouse, looking as sexy as ever and smiling. Then she drew out a long knife from behind her back with her right arm.

The first Ghanaian slave was slit quickly from pubis to sternum - not deep enough for his guts to fall out, but enough for him to shy backwards. As he did so, he fell overboard; the forty feet to the water did not kill him, but the blood in the water would.

The next got a crossways cut across the stomach, deep enough to slice the muscle. As he fell back over the side, his entrails began to squirt from his body. Others were offered weights to hold. A few grabbed them - one jumped over the side before being cut open and the rest were instructed to watch. He went down fast, entering the water with almost no splash. As he went deeper he did not exhale, but the pressure grew until he could bear it no longer. Letting go of the weight meant rising and fighting to get a fresh lung full of air.

Once he surfaced, he saw the carnage of the bodies; sharks had come to the party. He swam for his life, but to where? No matter how hard he swam, terror and death were only prolonged. The rest opted for the knife; the cuts became smaller and more intricate as Ciao Bella moved along her version of death row.

The two agents from the USA were last of course; they had never witnessed anything like this before and knew they never would again. Assigned to their fate, they waited. The cuts they both received were to the biceps. There was no defence, no plea for clemency, as they knew none would be given. Each went over the side of the vessel hoping to hit another person, or a shark head on. If one, at least, was lucky, his neck would break or the spinal cord be severed and then all would be dark. The cut to the biceps was extremely cruel: the arm could not be pulled backwards or pushed forwards from the shoulder, so no purchase in the water could be made, and no defence could be attempted. All they could do in reality was tread water, as limbs were taken by the deadly fish until it all ended.

A few hours later the captain lowered his three black balls from the mast, signifying the vessel was dead in the water, drifting without power. He telegraphed the engine room for two thirds revolutions forward and the four hundred and fifty foot long vessel began to make headway. The oil burners changed the water in her boilers to pressurised steam, which turned the turbine blades anchored to the central shaft of the engine. This spun the electrical generators for on-board equipment and the shaft also spun a reduction gear. At fifty revolutions per minute, the prop shaft spun the propeller to make eight and three-quarter knots. By the time the vessel had moved twenty feet, the sharks were dispersing and there was just a shade of rose pink left in the water. It matched her lips, but completely disappeared as soon as the propeller caught the discolouration of the sea water. No evidence would ever be seen; the ship's own charts and logs did not have an entry. The vessel steamed due west through the Mediterranean sea, heading towards the Strait of Gibraltar to turn south in the Atlantic and head off to Ghana to pick up another group of firm, healthy men to work to death.

This bit of fun would be over for a while.

"Oh what a shame," ran through Ciao Bella's mind. Her report to Robrotski was simple enough, sent by radio and then by telex to his then location. There was no need for code. It read: "Our guests have transferred to new location. The Emperor's clothing is still visible!"

Chapter 8: Wing Commander Butler

Beetle rallied the men he knew and trusted from the Rheims Negotiations in 1945. His men to hand from the military pleaded with the French, Italian, West Germans, the British and Soviets to come and talk. Weeks went by as each of the countries gradually revealed their hand. Their knowledge and the fact that they, too, were missing personnel, made grave their concerns, but they were all still in the dark. What direction could they take? Could they work together? Who would run the operation and how could they keep it secure? Heads of governments would need to be consulted on this, and it was going to take a blinking eternity.

There was no brandy and no cigars at this party until a lively ex-wing commander butted in. "Excuse me chaps, I just wanted to ask: if we struggle to trust each other, then who is there that we all trust? Just a question. Any thoughts?" He twiddled his classic RAF officer's moustache; his hair had greyed a little, but he was still athletic and now married with a second child on the way.

The highly positioned men who filled the room murmured and muttered away, and then Wing Commander Jack Butler butted in again. "Right, gentlemen. I have a thought." He stoked his pipe, standing in the ornate room in his civilian clothes, and said, "I need to make a few statements without interruption, then I will leave the room and allow you to talk amongst yourselves. I do believe I have a solution, but you will have to suggest it to me! Then I think there is a way forward!"

He paused and waited for them all to settle and the murmurs to stop. Eventually the room fell silent and he started. His baritone voice began, filled with vibrant authority. He knew his stuff inside out, back to front and upside down; they were going to listen as they had never listened before. The information he was about to divulge was going to send these men, who thought they were in intelligence, to a place in their own heads that enlightened them enough to realise they were not!

"Gentlemen I am going to read you a number of statements," said Butler. Statement one: FBI requests MI5, as they are unable to work outside the USA, to stop Glen Miller arriving Paris December 17th,

1944. Reason: if he arrives, will the troops' drive forward to German territory fail because the troops may party? Solution required."

Jaws dropped; there were gasps for air by nearly all attending, and the caller of the meeting, Beetle, nearly choked on his strong black coffee and thought, "Bloody hell; could that have been sabotage or even murder."

"Statement two: Italian Mafia! Benjamin 'Bugsy' Siegel, June 20th, 1947, shot from outside his friend's house while perusing his newspaper. Taken down with a high-powered rifle. The shot was taken from an unknown distance by an unknown person or assassin; one projectile through the heart and one through the head in quick succession. One presumes a professional engagement, on a man who could not be touched by the authorities."

In the stunned silence that followed, nobody moved; each man present waited for the blow to be from his own country!

"Statement three: Australia. 'Taman Shud', or 'Somerton Man', December 1st, 1948. Murdered by an unknown poison. No suspects found!"

Still silence in the room.

"Statement four: Japan, August 17th, 1949. Train derailed near Matsukawa by sabotage. Need I go on gentlemen?" Wing Commander Jack Butler strolled out of the room and said out loud, "None of the afore-mentioned have ever been admitted to by those responsible, or solved as a case, to this day." He closed the door behind him. He smiled gently to himself, not needing to wonder about the commotion inside the secret meeting with these respected gentlemen.

Inside the room, all the men looked at each other in astonishment and then turned to the one Israeli who represented Mossad. He looked at his accusers, shrugged his shoulders and said in his clipped English, "Is not us!"

Again they all looked at each other with suspicion and wondered what the bloody hell Jack ruddy Butler knew that they did not. He was called back in after a few hours. During this time he had been calmly eating lunch.

The self-elected spokesman from the Soviet Union asked with a heavy accent, "What else do you know that we of intelligence do not?"

Butler answered slowly and succinctly, "Sadly, men, I know the answers. Each of your governments has, at times - and I am sure will in the future require - an indisputably independent service. At this juncture I believe this is our only safe option: as independent states we can each authorise and agree our own plan of attack. The commissioned independent team can be seen as disposable, if need be. Any and all reports are to be distributed to all in this room and nobody is to be kept in the dark. If this is true, as I suggest, we need a team that has access to all continents with absolute anonymity.

"If you go to your superiors and go through my suggestion using my name, I believe you will be given positive feedback." Butler re-stoked his pipe, picked up his overcoat and hat and turned to leave the dim, smoky room. As he reached the door he turned, looked at all the faces then around the room and stated, "You have my contact details!" Then he walked through the open door and gently closed it behind himself. He smiled to himself and wondered what he had let the lady in for this time. He knew the other missions were justified and would never ask if he thought they were vengeful. This, though, was going to put her skills to the test and how the hell was he going to get her away from reporting for The Times? What would Fleming think when he realised who she really was? Now that was food for thought!

Chapter 9: Presence Required

Two months passed as each of the security agencies beavered away at their own investigations.

The Australians and British pushed on with their nuclear tests at Emu Field in the desert known as Operation Totem in South Australia. Five hundred miles south of Adelaide, the two tests went ahead as planned. Just a little enriched uranium-252 had gone missing. It had been taken by a physicist and passed on to a mule. The mule had no real idea of what was being smuggled out of Australia; he kept the package, as it had been given to him, by his side on the ocean liner. All the same, he did become really quite ill, passing on the package to his handlers in Egypt then dying of radiation poisoning. Nobody was any the wiser; another clue had slipped through the intelligence agencies hands. The package was then transferred to another courier and sailed by ship through the Suez Canal, on into the Mediterranean and then to the location of the final courier, making the last pickup in Venice. The cargo then found its way to Robrotski's lair.

In the meantime, the Americans had a similar experience, losing a similar amount of product at the Nye County, Nevada tests in January, 1951. The tests were only sixty five miles from Las Vegas and the exit route was simple for these couriers. Their contact time was much less and so their demise took a lot longer. They were in it for money and to gamble, knowing not what they were carrying or the risks. All the same, it took its toll on their bodies.

In the Urals at Totsk, the Russians had the same thing happen right under their noses; military security and scientists watched it all happen in front of their eyes. Not understanding the simplicity of the scam, it left them none the wiser - but a little short of product!

The Japanese were still trying to figure things out. Beetle was attempting to work out who, and at what level - if it was for real - had signed off Glen Miller's ticket.

The French were in the same boat. Their other concern was the organisation which had taken a lease on the submarine pens at Brest, with almost instant access to the Atlantic. The company was very secretive in odd ways - a little more than industrial espionage concerns would require.

Nothing much seemed to happen there and it was obviously not a fully commercial venture. Some private or independent work went in from independent companies, although most of the work that went on there was the re-fitting of Liberty ships purchased from the US as surplus, and so cheap. The company who had the lease of the submarine pens owned these vessels. The employees seemed to be happy but were so well vetted prior to employment that the French could not get one of their own men in. Most of the employees doing the real engineering work seemed to be migrants from the north and lived within the complex. These workers never seemed to come out of the complex and spend their earnings in Brest. Every time the French tried to get a person on to the workforce they failed. It became such a concern that ministers from Paris started to get involved. They would come, be shown around the complex and leave, seemingly quite happy with what they had seen - or at least thought they had seen.

The building of the new nuclear power plant in the USSR at Obninsk was running well on schedule and the builders were happy with progress. The Englishmen who came over from the UK were happy too. Everything was going to plan and measured up just right. This venture was going to bring the world just a bit closer together.

*

Berty and Murtyl had had their time off and she had been away reporting on another international motor race within Europe. Her report going into The Times was perfectly normal. Before returning to the UK, she had received a telegram from Berty saying they had a great opportunity to drop by to see a friend of his, from his youth. They met in Antibes, a little east of Cannes in the south of France. The chap she was introduced to was French, an ex-naval officer by the name of Jacques. He had been involved with a guy called Gagnan and they had patented a demand air breathing valve that could be connected to pressurised air tanks. He had been well decorated during the war for his exploits, even though his brother had been sentenced for being a collaborator. Jacques was excited to get Murtyl's opinion on this apparatus. It was selling in French speaking countries but they were struggling to make sales in English speaking countries. Names such as 'Air Liquid' just were not hitting the mark.

They dived together; Berty and Murtyl were impressed with the freedom of movement allowed by this equipment. Due to the relatively low pressure that could be held in the air tanks of the day, roughly seventeen atmospheres of pressure in dives of thirty minutes at a depth of five fathoms were all that could be achieved. Jacques and Gagnan were working on this. All the same, going into the depths without diving suits and bulky diving helmets was just incredible. Re-breathing systems were small but very dangerous and this was just a revelation. As the two of them were leaving Antibes after wining, dining, diving and relaxing in the wonderful picturesque port, they asked when Jacques would be able to deliver three or four sets to them. They also wanted a dry air compressor so they could charge the air tanks safely between dives. At that they left and returned to Dole with their sun tans topped up.

Arriving in Dole, Cash 'Charles' greeted them with the usual enthusiasm; they all feasted on local produce and a little red wine, reporting on the happenings of the last few weeks, discussing new ideas and possible new ventures. They sat in the candlelight, hidden away in the same place that Murtyl had found Berty again during the war, just those few years before. They laughed and joked – then Cash came out with a message from the baker in town. It was in English and was addressed to Murtyl:

Presence required.

Contact ASAP.

W.C.

Berty looked at Murtyl's face and commented in his still slightly Marseilles French accent, "It would seem your services, or ours, are required. I told you not to be impatient!"

Her reply was, "Wing Commander Butler would like me to report asap. I will call him in the morning as it is too late now to start and travel. There are no telephones that can easily be used at this time of night and he would have found us in Antibes if it was that urgent. So it is either nothing or it happens to be big and slow! But we're working again. Fantastic!"

Charles and Berty both agreed and all went off to bed straight away for an early start. At five thirty the next morning they were up and packing the reliable little Citroën Travant. By seven o'clock, Murtyl and Berty were on their way toward Calais: roughly four hundred miles on not the best of roads - but they were on their way.

They travelled from Dole to Dijon on the N5, staying on the road to Châtillon, where they picked up the N72 to reach Troyes. From there, the trusty Citroën journeyed along the N19 to Méry and on to Sézanne, then through to Monmirail and Château-Thierry on the N373. Finally they picked up the N37 to Soissons, then the N31 to Compiegne; the N35 to Amiens then the final leg which would take them to Calais via the N16.

By the evening they were in sight of the port and hoping to catch a ferry, and by midnight they were bedded down in a little bed and breakfast ten miles inland from Dover, having crossed by quite a rough channel.

At six o'clock the next morning, Murtyl was in a public telephone kiosk talking to her old friend and ranking superior Jack Butler, trying to find out what was going on.

He answered the phone and after the quick but polite greetings said, "There's a situation, Sweetheart. I think you and your team are the best bet, and you know how I don't like asking you to pick up where others are failing."

"Yes I know," she replied, "but if it's stimulating or is within the remit I gave you a long time ago, then I'm in!"

He countered with, "Great, but we're going to have to come clean with The

Times. This may take a while; it's not going to be 'in and out in a week and nobody any the wiser'!"

"OK Jack, I understand. I'll think it over as we drive up. Where do we meet this time?"

"Lady M, take your time. Now I know you're on the way, I have a few calls to make myself, reports to collect and information to gather then agree upon. I will see you at Peterborough railway station: southbound platform, first class carriage, 0745 hundred hours, London train, two days."

Her reply was military in manner: "Yes sir!"

The handset of the phone went down and rested back in its cradle. Murtyl turned and walked out of the red Post Office kiosk, looking concerned and rubbing her hands as if they were cold. She announced to Berty with great enthusiasm that they had two days to bugger about before she was to meet with the wing commander. As far as she was concerned, she expected him to be by her side during the meeting and suggested they went straight to London, and then enjoy themselves. In two days' time they could catch the Edinburgh early express train north as far as Peterborough, alight from the locomotive, change platforms then head straight back with Jack Butler. The initial brief and request would be gone through, and then they could see what was requested or what they were up against this time.

It was roughly only seventy miles to London and they were in the Ritz within three hours, eating a late breakfast and organising a room overlooking Green Park, the hotel being situated on the corner of Piccadilly Road and Arlington Street in the centre of London. There would be a little shopping to be done, a club or two to visit and time to generally put on a little weight. You never knew what the new job might entail; a little extra fat would probably be gone in no time.

The concierge recognised Murtyl as she walked into the Ritz - or actually, the doorman had recognised her and tipped off the concierge as to who she was. One of the owners of the establishment had had a few dealings with Murtyl in the past, and it was understood (although unofficially) that if she appeared and there was a room available, it was hers; no bill, no questions, no fuss. If she visited, Murtyl got whatever she required. Being the lady she was, not even Berty knew why this was the case, but he did know that she would never abuse or overindulge in this arrangement - which was for life. Only if she had business in London would she drop in to the Ritz and then never more than for a day or two. If she was working, this hospitality was not used, just in case it later reflected on the establishment.

Out of enthusiasm they discussed the flying kite that Charlie and Berty had built. They had tested it together and were now looking for way to communicate from a distance, ship to shore, as it were. The only way it was going to work, was if Charlie worked on some of the micro switches they had discussed. The base station could work from a mains power supply, a car or some other type of generator, whereas the person in flight had weight to worry about. Batteries were heavy and so the smallest possible was to be used. It could be on standby for periods of time to listen but it was agreed in the end that the pilot would send a message to the listening ground crew who would be on standby. That way, the two-way communicator in the air would only need to be live when required - saving huge amounts of energy.

The two days of fun and sightseeing in the new London that was changing, now that the city was being reconstructed after the war, had been interesting. Things were taking shape. Rationing was still in place but anything could be acquired if you knew where to look, knew the right person or had the cash!

The early steam train from King's Cross to Edinburgh chuffed and pulled her way out of London. She would be dropping the pair off at Peterborough in plenty of time to change platforms and head south, back to the city again with Jack.

It was a warm morning with no breeze at all. At Peterborough, the steam and soot hung heavy in the air around the platform; the damp was getting into their clothes and making it feel much cooler than it actually was. Murtyl took her right index finger and licked her finger end, quite sensuously. She put it to her lips as if to say to Berty, "Shhh." She moved forward gently until her hand and finger were close to Berty's face. His hair was swept back under the hat he wore – a felt, fawn trilby with a dark brown ribbon wrapped around it. His face was young, rugged and handsome. He was well shaved and still wrinkle free. He smiled at her and wondered what she was about to do. He felt a little self-conscious in his grey pinstripe suit with its double-breasted jacket and black polished brogues. He knew it was the fashion, but it was not his style. He could not think what could be out of place.

Murtyl winked and then drew her dampened index finger down across his face and said, "There, that's better! Now when we find Jack, remember: let him do the talking. This is his request and not an opportunity to talk about old times and past fun. OK?"

Berty replied in his slight French accent, "As you choose. I will talk only when required; it is your show!" He looked her up and down: her heels were just over an inch, so her total height was perhaps five feet eight inches. Her slim ankles almost grew out of the clean, polished, Cuban heeled ankle boots. They rose and widened just the right amount for the calves to be accentuated and then on to those beautifully balanced knees, which were hidden under her pleated black and cream skirt. Clinging to her slim waist and dropping down over the top part of the skirt, her cashmere pullover rounded out over her hips. As his eyes wandered a little further up, her torso began to broaden out with her ribs. Her breasts confidently held their proud position under her pullover, and the v-shaped neck of that garment dived down to emphasise their confidence. Her blouse rose up around her neck with the top two buttons left undone. It was white and under the collar around her slim neck was a half-inch deep band, made of black silk, acting almost as a choker. Her hair fell in soft waves around her face and then over her shoulders. It was not the fashion - it was pure style. Her crystal blue eyes shone and twinkled like the waters of the Maldives and looked right at him. Her eyebrows were strong and straight, the nose delicate, slim and strong with a light touch of makeup. A slight redness to her lips revealed their sensuousness. She smiled at him, showing the little dimples in her cheeks and those perfect white teeth. He knew they were special together; that he trusted her with his life - and she was the perfect killing machine.

A howling steam whistle from the

incoming train brought him back instantly from the wandering places in his mind. The platform guard blew his little pea whistle, asking everybody to stand clear as the great steam locomotive came to rest by the platform. The doors to the carriages were flung open a by the few passengers who were alighting, and the two of them stepped up through the open door of a carriage and closed it behind them. It was a second class carriage and they started to make their way forward though the train. More doors slammed closed, whistles blew and the iron horse started to chuff and thunder her way out of the station and onto the open rails toward King's Cross.

The two of them strode through the train towards the first class carriage and their friend, Jack Butler. Good old Wing

Commander Butler sat in a private section of the carriage with its own sliding glass partition, his pilot's brown leather briefcase by his side on the seat next to him. His suitcase was stowed above him on the rack, with just enough packed inside to last him three or four days. He preferred not to leave North Yorkshire wherever possible and going to the city was a trial in itself. Even his wife could not get him to do this; he only travelled when it was a request from his superiors, who in truth were few. He could run everything he needed to, by keeping his finger on the pulse from his office in Elvington, just a few miles from his home in York, where his two children and his best friend, his wife, remained. They were all that mattered to him - other than the two people he was just about to meet again.

Murtyl and Berty were old, trusted friends who had the skills he needed.

Wing Commander Butler was still of sturdy build, broad shouldered and round headed. His short-cropped, almost jet black hair was beginning to show a little steel grey. He looked up just as his friends saw him through the sliding glass partition. They all smiled and, when the door slid open, Murtyl entered, followed by Berty and Jack stood up. They hugged and greeted each other, then Jack burst out laughing, pointing at Berty. Tears of mirth started from his eyes and ran down over his naturally tanned skin. Berty looked at him in bemusement and wonder.

Murtyl smiled at Jack and said, "Twenty minutes. Never noticed the odd looks he was getting. Probably thought he was looking rather dapper, rather than like an American Red Indian."

Berty turned to look at his reflection in the glass and could now see what she had done. The soot from the steam engine was lightly deposited on his face; it was the same for everybody. But bloody Murtyl, with that index finger of hers, had drawn a line or two across his face in the soot. He started to laugh too then wiped his face clean with a crisp, white handkerchief.

The ticket collector came by, checked that all their tickets were in order and took an order for coffee and a light breakfast to the galley for the waiter. This was delivered and that then gave them an hour and a half to get down to business.

"By the way, Murtyl," said Jack, "you look astoundingly stunning. I just wish my wife, whom I love dearly, could carry off that style you just bloody well ooze. Yorkshire misses you and you are just going to have to give her more time in the future."

Murtyl replied, "Thank you Jack, I will as soon as time allows. Now stop beating around the bush and get on with it!"

Jack opened his briefcase and pulled out several files, all marked 'Top Secret'. He placed his hands on them, then looked at Murtyl and said in a very grave voice, "Before we start. What we know is very little, if anything. My belief is that this is probably a global thing. If I am correct and it is what it could be - which we don't know, of course - then it's big; bigger than you've ever been involved in before. I have permission from the top to let you loose – but if you are willing to take this on, you must understand: there will be no fall back, no help - you will be on your own. You will be classed as disposable; even friendlies must be classed as non-friendly. You will be totally independent. But you will report to me when you can. A meeting was held a few months ago in Paris called by General Walter B. Smith, now heading up the CIA."

Murtyl replied, "Yes I know him."

Jack smiled and said, "Yes I'm aware that you know a few others out there and they occasionally make contact with you independently. Anyway Beetle is Eik and Teddy's preferred boy. He has had a premonition - a hunch, or something. Two men have gone missing in the field and we have no idea what's going on. The French have an issue, as do the Israelis, Australians, Germans and possibly others. You know the individual agencies are never going to pool stuff that well, and nobody is going to trust one country to do the deed as it were. At the meeting in Paris I suggested that a free, independent team of trusted people was brought in. I offered up a few mysteries that seemed to make them prick their ears up and left, right and centre, then left them to it."

"Come on Jack, what have you suggested?"

"Well, I mentioned Glenn Miller, the Taman Shud or Somerton cases, the Matsukawa sabotage and 'Bugsy' Siegel issues - or cases, depending on your point of view. No names were mentioned but there was absolute silence."

"I bet there was," said Murtyl. "Jack, I will not confirm or deny…"

Jack butted in, saying, "Lady I do

not want to know either; they are all unsolved issues. The various services know not who or how, and the mere suggestion that premiers of state could work above them was enough to convince them that I knew something they did not. Hence we are here. You say yes, and I will see Flem. I still don't believe he has read your file, which is why you are underworked!"

"Oh yes and overpaid, no doubt!" she answered without thought.

Jack chuckled. "So if you say yes, there is the possibility I will never see you again. But then there is also the possibility the whole thing is nothing. This morning I brief the Cabinet at Number Ten. If you are in, I will go and see Flem and have you released from his duties until the effort is over. Every organisation has given me a report; these are under my right hand."

He could see her eyes twinkling and darting from his to the stack of top secret reports. "I know you crave the excitement. I can see you are interested, but lady you really have to remember there is going to be no help or cavalry to come to the rescue. If you're in, you're in, there's no getting out until it is over."

"Perfect, that's how I like it! Slide those files over here and relax; still your mind for your meeting and leave it with me. I will keep you apprised of progress, but not plans. Do I have open permission to do what I believe is right, or do you need to have prisoners as well as evidence? It's just that prisoners are a danger to progress, and may cause other issues!" Murtyl retorted.

"Right, start with the files. Where

are you staying so I can catch up with you in a day or so after I have had today's meeting? He paused for a second as his mind turned over options and then said, "Do you want to be at my meeting with Flem?"

"No Jack there is no need. We are at the Ritz. I will start to look into a few things but will not do anything until you confirm complete freedom from all authority. I understand your concerns about being disposable, but I think that gives us the sharpness, the edge and allows complete freedom from bureaucracy!"

"Yes and you do just love the adrenalin!" replied Jack.

There was silence in the compartment, except for the clackety-clack of the steel wheels rolling over the joints in the rail tracks.

Chapter 10: A Meeting with Winnie

Jack made his way by taxi to Number 10, Downing Street. His meeting was with the man in his third term as prime minister and leader of the Conservative Party. The big, burly man sat at his desk with his now famous great cigar smouldering between the fingers of his right hand. Winston Churchill rose from behind his desk and walked over to Jack as he entered the office. Jack was welcomed with a big hug. Coffee was brought into the room and they sat with the great desk between them. Sir Winston listened intently to Jack as he gave a verbal of Paris. Sir Winston had seen the written report, talked to several others including his counterparts in the USSR, USA, France and so on.

He also had on his desk a report that was personal from Vera Atkins of the now disbanded Special Operations Executive. He had read this report and knew of Murtyl; they had never actually met but he had followed her exploits towards the end of World War II and knew of her abilities. He did not, however, know too much about her present employment.

After the general six to seven minutes of pleasantries, 'Winnie' Churchill wanted to get into depth. They had ten minutes prior to the cabinet meeting and he wanted to get on with things. "So Jack, is she all I believe she is? Is she disposable and if there is a risk to national security, or international peace is she the girl?"

"I believe so sir," replied Jack.

"Why?"

"Well, sir…"

"No, no, no, lad, there's no time to think; spit it out, spit it out!" Winnie's deep, authoritative voice boomed out. Then he leaned back in his leather upholstered chair and waited impatiently for Jack to get started.

"Sir, she is the one who can get behind the lines and look around. She will be given less intensive scrutiny just because she is a woman in a man's world. She is efficient, effective, bloody well decisive and takes no prisoners. She will shoot to kill without hesitation. If the case exists, she will find it, hunt it down and deal with it. Her team is ingenious, daring and will follow her to the grave, as would I, sir!" As Jack made the final part of the statement, his right hand slammed hard onto his chest where his heart was placed. A loud bang reverberated around the office.

Winnie smiled at Jack and said, "That will do for me, Jack; that kind of conviction from a Yorkshire man is good enough! Stay in here and ask for what you want. I will be ten minutes with the boys. There are no expenses to be talked through. Other heads of state have agreed to this, depending on the outcome of my meeting with you. In ten minutes you should have the green light. Tell the girl I want to see her when it's all over. Preferably alive. I prefer not to do business with the first loser. Winners are what matter, lad, winners." With that he strode out of his office and in to his meeting, leaving Jack to twiddle his thumbs in the prime minister's office.

A full twenty minutes passed before

Churchill strode back into his office and pulled out one of his Camacho Cuban cigars. He pulled it out of its protective tube and held it between his thumb and forefinger in his left hand, then passed it gently under his fine nostrils, drawing air into his vast chest through them. As his chest inflated, his waistcoat tightened and he gave that familiar, broad smile. As he exhaled he spouted the following words to Butler: "Son, she has a green light. You can wish her Godspeed on my behalf and tell her I expect to shake her hand on her return – but this time in Yorkshire."

"Sir." Jack rose to his feet and started to leave the room. As he did so, Churchill tapped him on the back. He blew a plume of pungent blue-grey smoke out of his mouth and said, "I met her once, you know. She is the bravest, most devious, tricky, gifted blighter I have ever had save my rump. Help her if you can – but from a distance!" Jack nodded and departed Number 10, Downing Street, wondering how in the hell had she met the bloody pm and when. He would, when this was all over, ask her – but that was for another day. Now he needed to make an appointment with Fleming to get Murtyl a sabbatical from the paper and then get in touch with her.

Not bothering with the tube system, he went straight for a cab, instructing the cabby to head for the Ritz. On arrival, and after the concierge had notified them of their guest, he was shown by the bellboy to the suite that Murtyl and Berty were in.

On entering the room, he saw Berty in his stockinged feet, his grey trousers to just above his waist supported by a grand set of braces. His collarless white shirt was open at the top by just two buttons, allowing his suntan to show that it was not just from the collar up. One hand held a shoe and the other hand was brushing vigorously over the fine leather. The shoe shone and glinted in the refracted sunlight.

Murtyl walked into the room from the bathroom, tucking her blouse inside the waistband of her brown corduroy trousers. She pulled a V-necked jumper over her head and flicked her long hair out from behind the collar. Smiling at Jack, she walked over and gave him a hug. He looked into her eyes, a tear trying to escape from above his bottom eyelid.

Before he had a chance to speak she said, "I've read the files, Jack. If there is a link I will find it. It could be nasty, so we are off tomorrow and I will do what I need to with regard to Grandma and tidy my affairs, as it were. If it goes wrong, look after her will you? I will be back here in three days then we move. I have telegrammed Erich and Stuart to place them on standby in case I or we need them. If you are able to give any support, do it through Charles. I will have a courier system set up that does not involve any organisation but my own. Now we'll go for a walk, eat and then on to a bar. I think we should celebrate life, the love of life and being together, for tomorrow we may die!' Jack still had his overcoat over his arm, and Berty was now holding the door open to the suite, dressed and ready to go. He did as was signalled and all three of them went out on the town for an excessive night out.

At two in the morning they split up. Jack Butler buried his head between his broad shoulders, wondering how he was going to get through the day if he ever sobered up. Berty was worse for wear but had gone on to good quality French red wine and was just compos mentis. Murtyl, however, had drunk Jack under the table, head to head, pint for pint and was still full of mischief. Bemused, Jack could not understand how her enthusiasm and constitution could hold together after such a heavy night, knowing what she would be doing that day and the possible dangers that lay ahead. Second to her, he was first loser and was concerned that this all might become personal rather than business. But then again, if she didn't take her life style to heart, she wouldn't be the formidable person she was or have the team she had! He was still going to worry every minute of every sodding day about her. He felt sick and made his way to his slightly more humble accommodation.

Murtyl and Berty were at King's Cross at seven o'clock that morning and away on the Edinburgh Express. At Peterborough she alighted from the train and made a call to The Wheat, asking the landlord to let Gran know that she and Berty would be arriving that day, staying for two days, and to get the bar open early this night. Then back onto the train, getting off at Darlington Station, home of railways, and then catching a local engine to Yarm. The landlord of The Wheat had sent the baker with his van to pick them up from the station at Yarm and they were with

Grandma and their friends in next to no time. Hugs all round and lots of smiles later, they retired to Gran's home. Berty remained in the pub, playing cards. Later he would be locked out of the house for the night and would have to sleep in the pub when it came to bedtime.

Gran had stayed off the sherry after a few and was quite sober; she had a bone to pick with Murtyl and she wasn't going to wait. "Right, young lady, now that everybody has had their fill you can sit down and tell me what's going on! You never turn up out of the blue, without so much as a letter or card giving me some degree of notice. I could have had a gentleman friend here and been caught in an embarrassing situation!"

Murtyl burst out laughing, but Gran

stamped her foot, her right hand wagging and her forefinger pointing at her granddaughter. "You cheeky young wench, you can stop sniggering right now!" Her grey and white checked pinafore was spattered with flour from baking pies and cakes from the minute she knew they were on their way up to visit. Her real disappointment was that they did not visit often enough. The last time had been during those bitter cold dark nights around Christmas and the New Year. That was several months since and she missed the only relative she had left. The village looked after her and she played her part too in village life, but she did miss having this little cheeky bugger around to love.

As Murtyl's tears began to subside from laughing at her Gran and she was able to stand even with aching sides, she walked over to her gran, gave her a big hug, which made clouds of baking flour dance off her, and said, "I love you too, you old bat!"

Gran looked her only granddaughter up and down and asked, "What have you got yourself into, young lady? You never turn up like this and my sources say you're going to see Ron tomorrow. That spells trouble to me, so spit it out before I beat it out of you!"

The reply came back honestly and succinctly: "Gran, I really don't know at present what it's all about. I know it's important; I have given my word and that is all I'm able to tell you. I will be away for a while and will, I promise, contact you when I can. I will do it as Dad did. You know the drill: a post card or letter or two. One will be for you and one will be misspelled. The ministry men will pick that up! It may be nothing as yet, so don't you worry, it will all come out in the wash. I need to see Ron for my own peace of mind. I love this, you, and life too much to consider not coming back!"

"Oh my God, you're going behind enemy lines again, aren't you?"

"Yes Gran," Murtyl replied.

They hugged again and this time Gran's eyes spouted sparkling tears than ran down her face, picking up powder from her cheeks on the way and eventually depositing their cargo on Murtyl's blouse, making a right bloody mess.

"Is Dad's old bike good to go? I want to use it to go and see Ron and then go fishing with Berty. Just a few smells and pictures to remind me of home and you. Is trout OK for tea tomorrow?

"Yes and yes, but I hope you're not going poaching again. Kev's retired now you know!"

"I know, bless him, but there's no fun if it's not a bit of a challenge!"

"Your dad would be proud of you Missy, just as I am. Now sleep, eh?"

Chapter 11: Blyth & Partners

The next morning Murtyl was up with the lark, sleeves rolled up and out with her father's old bike. She pushed it through the archway by the pub and had a look through the window: yes, Berty was there, crashed out! She turned the fuel on and tickled the carbs, flooding the float bowls with fuel. She tied her hair up, looked up at the blue sky and popped her flat cap on with the peak toward to rear. Her goggles were resting on her forehead with the elastic stretching around the back of her head. Her brogues were on her feet and her brown corduroy trouser legs were tucked into her socks. Even though it was going to be a warm day, she wore a thick woollen jumper over her checked shirt. Knowing her weight was slight, starting the old Brough from cold when it had not been run since last summer would be a challenge.

She pushed the one hundred mile per hour 100 mph motorcycle down the hill a little. The ignition turned on, she left the beast in neutral. Picking up speed, she leapt on, sitting side saddle. More speed developed as she headed down the bank towards the church. Her right leg came over the bike and flipped the gear lever up after dragging in the clutch with her left hand. The clutch was engaged as she dropped all her weight hard over the rear end of the bike. Number 1 piston came on its compression cycle but she had the decompression valve open to allow the motor to spin and give it time to gain oil pressure. When number 2 piston came up on its compression cycle for the second time, the mixture began to be ignited by the tiny blue spark being produced by the spark plug. The decompression lever was released and the massive V-twin motor burst into life. She popped the gearbox back into neutral and sat on the bike at the bottom of the hill, slowly revving the engine up and down from one thousand rpm to three thousand rpm, checking that it sounded correct and that the oil pressure warning light did not illuminate.

Once satisfied that all was in order, she rode up the other side of the small valley. At the top of the hill she applied the brakes, front and rear, gently, making sure they were working efficiently and the tyres had gained a little heat through the friction and stress on the tarmac. All this before this missile of a motorcycle was allowed to breathe life as its designers had hoped it would be.

Murtyl smiled to herself, and thought, "Good old girl. Stokesley to warm up; fuel up then we'd better get off and catch Ronny in Yarm." She pushed the bike hard, as was her way, and was outside Ron's office in Yarm just five minutes before nine o'clock. The bike was on its stand, her cap was in her pocket and the goggles were hung over the handlebars.

Ron tapped on the window and waved her into the building. On top of his leather inlaid desk, his file on her in was place. There were also two bone china cups and a pot of tea. He had greeted her with a warm but polite hug and his great broad smile, side parting strong on the left side of his head, hair dark and Brylcreemed in place. His sober, dark grey suit of the legal person toned everything down as was the legal profession's way. He guided Murtyl to a seat and she shook her head He went behind the desk and sat in his ageing leather high-backed chair. Clasping his hands and then placing them into an arch in front of his face, he started with, "I'll pour, you talk! Milk?"

"Yes Ron, milk is good. I need to go through a few things and make sure all is in order. You have my last diary and I now think that there may be reason to write another soon. I know you understand what the last one contains, and this could be similar. It is never to see the light of day, or be read unless I have implicitly instructed it to be otherwise. If I don't return, the diary you have now must be destroyed. Now I need to go through my estate, and then update you on a few things. Gran must be looked after no matter what the cost and so on."

"What have you signed up for now girl?" he said with a great sigh as she sipped at her tea.

"I've shaken hands Ron; that's all that matters. I've no idea what is what yet, I just need piece of mind that you know what's what."

"OK young lady, let's go through it all." Then he opened her file and they went through it page by page. At half past twelve, they left his office and went for lunch together.

Then they parted company. Murtyl was on her way on the Brough Superior and Ron returned to his office. His mind wandered as he thought about her; maybe one day, just maybe, she would settle and grow up. "And then again," he thought as he smiled to himself, "there's not a bloody hope in hell of that, is there? She's just nuts. Bloody brilliant, but just plain nuts!"

Riding out of Yarm, Murtyl's mind wandered and she started to think of an old friend from the village. Pete had been a few years older than her and by the time she was hitting fourteen he had gone to university to study Engineering. She had no idea if he had survived the war but knew he was to have taken over the family machining and fabrication business in Middlesbrough. It was a week day; Blyth & Partners must still be there near the transporter bridge. Why not go down and see if he was there? At least she would get to see what it was like down there over the border now. By the time she had stopped thinking about it, she was parked outside the massive old building. Some of the doors were open and she could see men working by their lathes and milling machines. As she entered the building through the main office entrance, a security guard asked her for identification. She was shocked and surprised by the request, not expecting it - particularly by a man who was actually armed and obviously military trained, even though he was in civilian clothes. Murtyl gave her details to both him and the young lady sitting behind the tired reception desk. With this sort of set up she was prepared to retire and head home. There must be reason for the security and it was not that important she saw Peter. It had been a long time and the world had changed immeasurably.

The slim, blond girl behind the shabby desk looked up and said that there was no answer from Peter's office or the board room. Would it be possible for Murtyl to leave her contact details? These would be passed on to Mr. Blyth. This was done and Murtyl was just leaving by the main entrance, escorted by the security guard, when in a great roar, like a clap of thunder, Peter bounced down the foyer.

"By the Gods, is that you? Damned if it's not Murtyl. What in Hades are you doing here?" he boomed. The guard and Murtyl spun on the balls of their feet. They both turned in unison, in crisp, military style. The security guard looked at Mr. Blyth with that, 'I'm only doing my job sir' look in his eyes. Murtyl looked up at this great man and smiled that warm, bloody-good-to-see-you smile. Peter stood there in his three piece suit - all six foot two, eighteen, perhaps twenty stone of him. His hair had thinned, or maybe, to be fair, bolted. His teeth had not changed; they were just as she remembered them. His nose was broad at the bridge and had obviously been scrumming in rugby but his smile was a lump broader. He had his mother's smile. Even at this monstrous size he looked bloody fit; maybe he still played the gentleman's game. His raised his arms, beckoning her to go up the stairs and meet him on the landing. As she jogged up the stairs, she noted the cut of his suit. It was Oxford, Cambridge, civil servant style. Not too modern, but conservative, in that 'I'm part of the establishment' style. As she got closer, she realised he must have grown a bit more since she had last seen him in the village before the war. Her head came only partway up his chest. He bent slightly and politely, then picked her up and gave her that 'I know you' hug.

He whispered into her ear, "Thank God you're alive. I heard through the grapevine that some girl from where we come from had gone abroad during the bad times. I thought it could only be you. I visited your gran once a year or so during those dark days but she never gave me a clue. My office. Let's talk, and swap notes - at least as far as we can, eh?" He put her down and she followed him along a dark, wood-panelled corridor.

On entering Pete's rather grand office, which in reality suited his grand stature, Murtyl notice a most complicated model on a table near the window. In the office, a picture of Peter's father hung above a fireplace that was never used. The building must be heated in the winter as there were radiators, one on the wall under the table in front of the window and another on the opposite wall. The ceiling had a lot of fancy plaster work and a chandelier hung from the centre of it. There were two extra lights on the big man's desk to assist his work in the winter months. To one side was a draftsman's table that looked well-used. Yet her eye kept returning to the model.

She just had to ask: "Peter, what on earth is that model of?"

He replied with, "It's a bit of a well-kept secret, but not *that* well-kept and I know you will have signed that document.

Anyway you may be able to help me put one piece together with another. The large part of the model is the plant that Blyth & Partners are fabricating and producing. I still cannot get over the fact that we got the chance to tender for it. The skills are up here in the north and the wages are lower I suppose. We have a good record of staying on budget and surpassing quality control. Still, though, I feel it was a bit of a coup, considering all the other companies in the UK that must have gone for it. I didn't even know the project was on, never mind the fact it had a green light and is going ahead. Sorry, I digress. It is the guts of the nuclear power station that is to go on-line at Obninsk in two years' time. The Ruskies are building the exterior and the generator side of the plant, and here, we are building the reactor and turbines. There are completely new grades of metals arriving almost on a daily basis and we have to work out new ways of welding, stressing and machining them. The tolerances are not too much of a difficulty but converting measurements is a blinking nightmare. I have three guys just keeping an eye on that side of things. You know the old saying: measure twice and cut once. My guys are measuring thrice and then they check it again before cutting! No mistakes yet though so it's all going well."

"Wow! You must be chuffed to hell and back winning that, Pete. How did you get a sniff of the contract being up here?" Murtyl asked.

"Well I think there are several reasons: we are well known to Imperial Chemical Industries, or ICI, who are just down the road - and they do a bit with the Russians. The steel industry and its technical expertise is all around Redcar and we are pretty much on the river bank so there is easy access to shipping. As well as that, an old friend from my days at Oxford seems to be influential. I'm not saying anything underhand went on but Oxford Bob seems to know all the right people."

'Who the hell is Oxford Bob?" she asked.

"Oh just a smooth guy who was at Oxford at the same time I was. His name is Robinson but we called him Bob as he was always bobbing in and out of different ladies' homes, smooth sod! He is a well-to-do businessman and is involved with the civil service guys somehow. He suggested we meet and have a look at the project. He bought a few shares in Blyth & Partners on the understanding he would financially assist if we won the contract. The cunning bugger probably did the same with a few of the other companies who tendered, when I think about it. We are also fabricating some accelerator pipe for him but I honestly for the life of me have not worked out exactly how or where any of his businesses will use them!"

"How very fascinating. Come over for dinner tonight; I would love you to meet Berty and I am sure Gran would love to see you too. Seven o'clock good for you?"

Peter replied with little or no hesitation in his deep effortless voice, "Damned right I will!"

Chapter 12: Opening the Package

Nick had sweated hard over paperwork all day and done some odd jobs around the house. He too was on tenterhooks, clearing the decks as if he was getting everything shipshape for Murtyl, through her second diary, to take over his life. He just hoped that little Pip's world was not going to be turned upside down too. God forbid if it affected her schooling. It couldn't be helped if it did; he had struck a bargain with little Miss Busybody and Murtyl's greatest fan and there was no way he could go back on his word. He had decided, though, that they would only go through this diary together if he could get Pip to agree it would be Friday nights, Saturdays and Sunday during the day. It would kill them both to be that disciplined but that was how it would have to be!

Pip bounced through the unlocked front door after alighting from the school bus just a few yards from the entrance to the house. Her satchel was dumped on the floor and her shoes didn't get the chance to leave her little feet before they had arrived upstairs in her father's office. "Where is it Dad, Where? You haven't opened it, have you? You promised!" came out of her, during her first breath.

Nick stood his ground and looked at her with his 'calm down' eyes that exuded a look of 'you should trust me!' He opened his mouth and said, "You know the rules: shoes off at the door; coats and jackets hung up - and your little hat has a place too, I believe!"

"Yes, yes Dad, I know all that. But

this is a special day; I need to know!"

"Well stinky, if you had followed the rules you may have paused long enough to notice that the package is on the telephone stand, just below where you should have hung your stuff up. Patience, young lady, patience."

Little Pip darted out of the office and bounded back down the stairs. There it was, untouched: that precious parcel with – oh, it had to be - yes, it *had* to be the next diary. Grabbing it, she darted back up to the office where her father was still sitting.

He smiled at her and said, "Trust me young lady, we can open it together. If you remembered 'being aware of being aware', you would not have missed it! Now, come and sit by my desk and you can open the parcel."

Little Pip sat down as instructed, little grey skirt down to her knees, long white socks coming up to meet it. Her white school blouse was buttoned right up to the top and she wore a blue V-neck pullover over the top of it. She beamed at her dad, desperate to paw the brown paper off and see what the contents had in store for the two of them. The string was pulled away and the brown paper disintegrated, leaving a black, A4-size book. Most of the cover was clean and shiny; none of it was faded by sunlight, but a line of thick, grey-white dust showed along the length of it. There was one thumb print. A sheet of white paper sat on top with a hand written note from Ron Kirk. It read:

Dear Nick,

It's been a week or two since I have seen you. I could have telephoned

but I thought Pip would enjoy the excitement of this diary arriving

by post. Be diligent and keep your word: make her proud – from

what I remember, there is a lot to verify! You have your work cut out.

Call me if you need me!

Yours truly,

Ron.

Nick took a deep breath, as did Pip, and they opened the diary.

Nick looked at Pip and said, "Here we go Sweetheart. Page by page!"

Chapter 13: April, 1951

Have had a few meetings now with Jack and some files are to be handed over later today.

There has been a little trouble from work regarding my extracurricular activities. Seemingly, Mr. Fleming had originally been bullied into employing me by my previous employers. The file he was given had been 'mislaid' or at least not studied, therefore he had remained unaware of my previous activities. So much for the M.I.'s, I think! Anyway I digress. Once the files were in my possession, Bert and I headed off to Dole to study them before deciding on the best modus operandi.

Have decided to start with a three-pronged investigation.

Erich has a remit to investigate through contacts the top twenty new companies since World War II. This will be done initially through the banks in Zurich then he can do some digging with Stuart.

Bert and I flew to Quebec and then travelled by car into the USA to try and pick up on the two files from the American agents. Several firms have been buying oil fields and large shares in companies that own the rights to various oil fields, primarily around Long Island. Digging the paper work back, things keep leading to several organisations that were not in existence pre-World War II. So we headed out to the fields to do a little on-site digging. Berty needed to get heavily involved as a French-Canadian; these arrogant bastards prefer that the little lady is seen and not heard. The odd thing that was noticed: certain people, whom we never had the chance to talk to, seemed to appear and re-appear in the distance. We never came close enough to be introduced but the stature of one was memorable. I got a photograph of the pair but there was no identification to be had through Jack, once a copy was sent to him in the UK.

We left the USA to return to Europe once I had employed the Pinkerton Agency to follow up a few things that needed to be done. The promise of the other files from different governments meant that we could look at this in a bigger frame. The Pinkerton Agency also had enough personnel to be able to rotate or watch each other for security purposes. We still had no idea what had happened to the FBI boys - why they had gone missing or what may have triggered them both to disappear at the same time. They must have been spotted, but what had alerted someone, or at least given them away - and who the 'someone' was - we had no idea.

Slowly slowly against an unknown enemy is not who I am. Stealth, yes. Invisibility, yes. Planning and knowledge is everything, and we knew nowt. We needed all the intelligence, however garbled, in one place to sift through and roll about in our minds. I needed to understand, find connections and link all the reports together. If there was a link, no matter how tenuous, there had to be a common denominator.

All the reports had arrived with Jack in the UK. Taking the files to Yorkshire would not be fair on Gran. The files needed to be split up and broken into several complex bundles, each bundle then to be sent by courier, parcel post and or by airmail to Charles, or at least various drop points for Charles to pick up from in France. That way it would be nigh on impossible to follow all the packages all the time, or when they arrived.

By the time we made it back to Dole, Charles had arranged a room for the three of us to work in. The parcels remained unopened until we arrived but the set-up was correct. The three walls without a door were now covered in blackboards; the aim was for us to each take a file and go through it. Each file was to get four two-hour study periods only. During the study period, notes and headings were to be made on the blackboards. At the end of the day, the blackboard would be rotated to leave a clean surface. Then the next file would be gone through and notes would be made the same way. Each of us went through each file. At the end of seven days and seven files each we could cross-reference each other's notes on each file, looking for coincidences or match-ups. As each of us is a different individual, we would naturally find some different things standing out; it was the oddities that I was looking for. Then we could cross-reference the final seven individual boards and see if there were any match-ups!

What a rubbish idea that turned out to be! Nearly ten days gone and the three of us were still picking through all these damned files. The theory had to be correct but nothing stood out. I took a day off in the

training room with Berty and we went at it.
Temper was always something I had
complete control of, but this was beginning
to get to me. We went out hunting to get a
breather and some well-deserved fresh air;
came back, ate - but I still needed to be out.
Berty and I left the grounds in the dark and
went into town for a glass of wine or two.
While sitting outside in a café, we chatted
about anything not connected with the case.

Then it struck me like a slap in the
face: this was peacetime, and we were
working as if it was not. Yes, there was the
odd policeman or gendarme walking by, but
life was going on all around. There was no
military presence and no one was suspect.
You just did your business plainly and out in
the open; as long as you did it with
confidence, authority and looked the part,

who was going to ask any questions? Half the records on anybody had been lost in those dark years, so you had to take some things on face value. It was time to go back and reassess those boards and get Erich and Stuart's findings into the mix.

The next day, a few things became a little less muddy. Just like hunting, you're not looking for the whole target and a full picture; you're looking for the movement - the shimmer of movement - that does not quite fit the pattern of the breeze through the grass. Then, if you're unlucky, it rips a claw across your face and you lose an eye. In this case we were fortunate: deep in the boiling mass of concentrated information on the blackboards, we kept coming back to the letters 'S' and 'R'. They were insignificant to us, but they were the only common thing on all the boards. I had no idea what for, or why, but there had to be something from ten days' effort.

The two lads arrived and after quite a few years of no reunion we had a good first night. Then we started to go through their work and there it bloody well was: SR Enterprises. Lots of different organisations feeding into it. Tentacles all over the world in different businesses. Starting with a healthy deposit, it had grown from 1946 into an international spider's web. No information was coming out of the banks but it tied all the boards together in a flash, from shipping, mining, transports, building, manufacturing - you name it, they were into it. Oil fields, oil production; government contracts - this couldn't happen unless you were well connected, you were dirty, or both.

Oh, the smell of dirt. My heart was bursting with the feeling that the hounds must have when they fall on that certain scent. Oh bugger - the chase was on!

The five of us sat down and started to produce a plan. I loathe plans that have no concrete end-date or finality, but the only way we were going to get to the bottom of this was to work as a coordinated team. It was agreed that we would slip into pairs and go after pre-agreed targets. If a target was verified and confirmed as linked into S R Enterprises, no matter how tenuous that link, that group was to back off and bring the information back. The last thing we needed was to trigger any alarm bells and have one or more of us go missing. There was no future in that! So Erich and Stuart went to Lloyds of London to look at new shipping companies; their registration, routes and insurances. There had to be an ounce of something there. They beat Bert and I back from the Middle East, where we looked for new oil production companies and found nothing. Royal Dutch Shell, British Petroleum and all the traditional big players were there but there were no really new boys in the game. It had been laborious and slow; no matter what angle was taken, there was nothing going on that was out of the ordinary.

We re-grouped and each team went off on a different tack. The boys were off to follow up on what had been learned at Lloyds regarding this shipping company. All the vessels were ex-Liberty ships; some had been refitted in France with new, state of the art diesel-electric propulsion systems.

Theoretically, these would save the shipping company money in bunker usage and the ability to make more speed. The costs involved against the long-term life of the vessel just did not weigh up. So the lads needed to try and get a job at the chosen re-fitter's yard. They were off!

Berty and I separated and started to look at cargo destinations, tonnage and back-haul cargoes. For any vessel - unless cargo specific ones such as oil tankers - there has never been the luxury of sailing in one direction with your holds empty. A shipping company would always try to get a ship a back-load or return load, at least in the return direction of the vessel, to make more money. Competition in shipping has always been fierce and it was just the way things were done. Most of these Liberty ships followed a fairly normal type of shipping route - except two. These two that did not had more erratic and oddball destinations. The cargo always looped back to the owners somehow and they were never fully laden according to their manifests. They had been the first two vessels to be fitted with the new propulsion systems. They carried fewer crew members as a result of less maintenance. They really did cover some distances and at sea averaged almost eighteen knots. Their crews did not change either, which was really curious. You may have heard of a sailor with a girl in every port, but whoever heard of a crew who did not want to have quality shore leave?

So we started to dig. One vessel sailed a regular route to Adelaide, Melbourne, Sydney, Brisbane in Australia,

*across to Japan, Nagasaki and Hiroshima,
and then to Shanghai in China and back to
Adelaide. The route was simple and the
trading of goods made sense. Except once,
when it veered off course and went missing
for five days - or at least turned up five days
behind its normal schedule. This had been
after leaving Brisbane. When she landed in
Japan, the captain had reported engine
trouble. Normal enough, until you start to
backlog all the information that we had
started to assemble over months. This one's
date was April 1953.*

*At the same time, one of the sister
ships that seemed to have a profitable route
from India, running with rice and spices to
Africa and sailing down into the
Mediterranean and then running back out
with Persian carpets to the UK and Holland,*

had gone missing for a similar period of time near India. Again nobody had questioned any of this. This particular vessel always carried less weight than the others so we nicknamed her the 'Shandyandy.'

So while the two lads pushed on to try and get an in at the port of Brest and then find a way further up the ladder without taking too many risks, we started to follow the Shandyandy. Nothing unusual was witnessed regarding dockers loading and unloading at any of the windswept ports. Some ports were rainy and wet; some were baked in burning sun, made even worse by the reflection of sunlight from the sea. But there were things to note: there were small amounts (small being one and two tons) of cargo that had not been loaded onto the ship in previous trips, but which seemed to come *off. For example, a part for a steam locomotive, loaded in Liverpool or Teesport and headed for India, arrived in India with no problem; it was just that the size and shape of that package had change quite considerably. Jumping to conclusions, it seemed that smuggling of some sort was probably going on. Yes, a concern but how did it fit in with our task? What the hell was going on?*

We were getting nowhere and months had now passed, and Jack, through the cartel of worried countries, started to lay a little pressure on. This came with a greater access to funding which was always going to help.

They had looked into the Brest operations run by the SR Enterprises group. It was more than just a closed shop; nobody really went in or came out. The personnel had arrived with the company and presumably would leave with the company. Ships came in from the company's fleet for work and went out. Customs saw manifests and somehow things were cleared and taxes paid. That paperwork took us nowhere either!

A few things started to hit the news that were interesting, as they seemed to start to help clear a smoke screen. At first it was just two things - but a pattern started to emerge.

Chapter 14: On the Liberty Ship

On January 27th, 1951, Frenchman Flat, in Nye County, Nevada, USA was blown away - quite literally blown away - by the United States Department of Energy in the first one kiloton nuclear test in that zone. Where Frenchman Flat had been was roughly sixty-five miles northwest of Las Vegas. This test, according to the world's press and the reports, had gone extremely well. The reported fallout, radiation and destruction had been as expected. However, some boffins were quietly in the background trying to make the argument, using their own theoretical mathematics and calculations, that this possibly was not the case. According to their calculations there could - or there should have been - a slightly bigger bang!

In our time not long after, but at the time a lot of dots had been joined together regarding the smuggling side of this operation. European precious metals were being hauled in under many guises and most of the time top dollar was being paid to small individuals. Dealing in bullion was at least a bit naughty. It was not what we were after, although during this time we had been for a swim...

The Atlantic is at best cold and in the winter, with high tides and high winds was not going to happen. The plan was as follows: Erich and Stuart had scouted and tried all they could to get into the old submarine pens at Brest, but to no avail. They then had started doing a little fishing from outside the pens, but the old German guard posts were manned. No guns were visible, but they were definitely watching from them. Weapons are easily concealed, so we just did not know. Our decision was to go in and have a nosey around. The fishing routine of every Saturday and Sunday night had been set up by the lads, taking the same roundabout route and trawling with lines off the stern. It would give us two hours tops to get in, out and rendezvous with the boys on their return leg. We used the tide just before it ebbed, going in and going out, to assist us getting out. It would help us save energy and so assist the dive time we had with Jacques' new Aqua-Lung. A glutton for adventure, he wanted to come and join us in the dive; just check out his military medal tally - several to him and none to me!

It was a full moon night with little cloud cover. Perfect; no light assistance was needed to get us to the pens. Bert and I took off our individual breathing sets and secured them to the steel climbing rings, just under the waterline. We went up and then removed our drysuits - leaving wet marks everywhere would be too easy for any sentries or guards to spot. On the return trip the drysuits could be sunk or weighted to the bottom.

This particular Liberty vessel had been in for her refit for around three weeks now. It was dark in the casemate of a concrete building, but once your eyes were accustomed to the light it was not too bad. The two of us were wary but we made it to the gangplank, looking for clues and guards while aiming to board the vessel. Work was being done to her deck in the middle between the accommodation block at her stern and the engine room and bridge structure midships. Berty headed straight for that area to get a look at what they might be trying to achieve.

In the meantime I went below deck. Emergency red lights were on so sight was no issue. Directions were more of a potential problem but I soon found my way to the engine room. Yes, there it was: a beautiful new electro-diesel, most of the way through fitting. Wow! I could have stood and simply admired it for hours but time was pressing. We were forty-five minutes into the agreed one hundred and twenty minute operation: move girl, move!

To the starboard side of the engine room there seemed to be normal hull plating, welded as the original designer had intended. To the port side however, a new structure had been put into place. It had its own entrance, which was inviting to an inquisitive girl like me. Opening and going through the watertight door allowed me to enter a space that had all its walls in place and a floor that was under construction, in the process of being double-plated and strengthened. At one end of the room a mounting was being welded in place to a bogie that rested on a set of tracks. Every five inches there were degree markings and halfway up the bulkheads were structures to support whatever was going to go in here. It was semi-circular but I surmised would be completed to a circle. It measured nearly three feet across and was obviously going to take some bloody weight. Twenty-five feet or so above all of this was a hole in the deck. I took images on some infra-red film with a little Zeiss camera to study later. It was time to get out.

Maybe Bert had found a few things - and maybe the bugger hadn't.

He was in the water waiting for me and we made our way out to the lads after sinking the dry suits. The tanks on the Aqua-Lungs were close to empty but they had done their job well. This was possibly the first mission a set had ever been on; I'd have to ask Jacques, if and when time permitted. We exited the area cleanly and all headed back to Dole in two separate cars. The film could be developed there and we could start to put a few more things together. It was about time some more things fell into place.

Charles developed the film from both our cameras as the rest of us slept. Mine came out as I described. We all studied them and then looked at Berty's frames. My first impression was that these were images you took on another trip. One image was of a tubular object with many spikes coming off it, as if it was an elongated mine - or a tree with most of its branches removed. On closer inspection each of the branches had capped ends and was directed slightly towards one end of the tube. His other images were of a foundry; granted it was a brand new foundry, but yes - that is what it was. He swore it was taken that night on that vessel. On about the fifth image there were some tell-tale markings visible in the background that confirmed it was the same vessel. The images also showed new living accommodation in one of the holds!

Now we had to work out the

significance of it all. Each of us had the whole case in our heads in our own individual style. Paper and pencil time, lads. The results soon came in.

Smelting on board a ship could only mean smuggling and that would account for some parts of cargo disappearing or at least changing shape and size. The Christmas tree shaped tube was a different matter. In the oil industry it can be a pressure branching and direction head for a well, but this had no capped end and was obviously going to be securely fitted to the boat's deck. Secondly, why would its elevation need to be adjustable? Time for a walk.

On my return I saw that everyone had been moving around and having a bit of a breather. The four guys looked at me as if I was an alien. I looked at them in the dim light; I had no idea what time of day or night it was. I was that dog tired, I couldn't remember if it was light or dark outside less than five minutes ago. I asked which one of them was going to spit it out. It was obvious they had come up with a theory and the way they looked at me meant I was the judge and jury.

Charles took the lead and started with a blank blackboard and started to draw. It was the Christmas tree. The base was drawn as if hinged and on a slider, which was the bogie I had seen. The top of the tree was flush, or almost flush with the deck, with an opening or hatch that could seal it off. Each of the branches coming off had wires leading from them to a clock with 'timer' written below it.

He looked at me and said, "You

better sit!"

I smiled and sat.

"An Accelerator gun! Elevation adjustment for distance. Fixed muzzle velocity. Set correctly, it could push a quarter-ton object - or at least lob it - into space. It would fall back to earth, impacting roughly one hundred and fifty miles away in the direction the weapon was pointed. After going through all your notes in the last eighteen months, my questions are: why were all those nuclear test yields possibly short of the mark? Who has been buying into oilfields hard? Where are the oilfields that they have bought into? When did those two vessels go AWOL?"

By now I was staring in amazement at Charles. "How does all this and *smuggling fit together?"*

He answered, "Ma Chérie irresistible, you have power, money and no chasers. You are not an organisation but an individual driven by greed, knowing nobody will ever bring you to book. You pay well and build a team of believers who will dance to your command. Buy legitimately precious metals in Europe, some stolen and some not. To treble plus its value, you need it away from Europe to say, India where no questions will be asked.

"To get heavy weights of it out of Europe, it must go by ship. Smelt, cast and paint as machinery and its out. Smelt it en route and pour ingots. Then sell - what could be easier? If I was still the person I once wanted to be, I could be trying to produce a nuclear warhead or two. Hard to

place them where you want to without being seen, but lobbed from a freighter one hundred and fifty miles offshore and you're home free. What could be to gain? You can't stand and watch that kind of display without dying. I don't drink any more, but I need wine now. I feel sick, and when that sinks in little lady, you will too!" He grabbed an open bottle of red wine, lifted it and started to pour it down his throat.

Taking the bottle from his lips and wiping them with his sleeve, he looked at me and said, "You have a little time. Not much, I know - but the world has not been held to ransom or blown up yet. SR must still need something. You have to get there before it or its employees do, then follow the thread back. Take the head off the snake, lady or the world changes for ever!" He held out the

255

bottle in his hand and proffered only one word: "Drink?"

I took the bottle, put its neck to my lips and then had a swig, looking at the others. They were all ashen white. My thoughts were now racing as to how close they were and to what had happened to Beetle's boys. Which of the other agencies had lost men for no apparent reason? Getting someone on the inside was not going to happen so it had to be a watching, preparation and possibly sabotage operation.

I told the lads to get some sleep, while I perused the blackboards. So if Charles was correct, which I hoped not, there had to be a pattern.

My chalked up ideas went as follows:
Uranium 235 = nuclear fission and

power / electricity

> *Uranium 235 (enriched) = nuclear bombs and explosion tests. Death and radiation (fallout)*
>
> *Smuggling = money*
>
> *Oil fields: the new money, the new power. In the last ten years, the world's oil production and use had doubled and that ever-increasing hunger was not going to slow. The curve was accelerating and production was set to double again in the next two years.*
>
> *I had never had a problem playing high risk or long odds if I felt I was in control or had enough information to give me a fighting chance. I'd gone up with the boys against a hundred well-trained, armed men who believed they were the best and we had proved them wrong. This was different;*

our adversary was working on several continents with a long-term goal. Erich had been right: we needed to find each starting point and follow it back to the head. On the way, lay and set snares and traps that could be sprung remotely.

Conclusion. That had to be it: high shares in, or control of, oil fields in production. Demolish competitors by lobbing nuclear devices on said competitors, clearing them out and making the areas radioactive and so no-go zones. Nobody need know, or could know, where the weapons had appeared from. Oil prices would go through the roof and you pretend to be nervous like everybody else. Perfect!

But not now. I rolled my sleeves up and went for a brisk walk before collapsing into bed. I needed a plan and we needed to *act upon that plan now!*

Chapter 15: The Plan

As ever, we would split into two teams. Both teams were to report to Charlie and Charlie would feed back to me with his assessment.

The boys, Erich and Stuart, were to go back through the shipping records of this organisation and visit any ports that were irregular or regularly visited but out of their own regular pattern. I knew that would sound daft but it was that hunting thing again.

In the meantime, it was for Bert and I to shake a tree or two in officialdom and get the maths checked out on these nuclear tests. Then work a way to steal from the test sites or from some part of the production procedure. Prove it could be done. At least then we would know if it could! That just might take us to a point where we would start to cross paths or tread on some toes in the SR network.

At the same time we needed to have a look at the possible or more probable smuggling and see how it was being done. Was it being done to part-finance the whole thing or was it being done because it could be? In other words, was it essential and could it be a weak link?

After several days, the boys were off to Ghana. They were on their own; communication from there was not going to happen quickly. The best that was going to happen was by telegram. They couldn't go direct to Charles; we'd be on the move so I had to reluctantly drag Jack in. At least it could go through his office and not involve his family. Bless him, he was only too happy to help and take the lead on any report going out to all parties.

Then I went through our thoughts and possibilities with Jack; he asked me to delay the next report until things had been verified. While doing this, Berty had worked on the communications issue and had come up with several sets of what in essence were portable longwave radio transmitter and receiver units. Not crystal clear and they took a bit of warming up but it did give direct communications. Sets were rigged up for Charles; a set in parts was sent out to the lads disguised as three separate wireless sets and Berty wired one direct into the little old faithful and reliable Citroën Travant. Once back in the UK he did the same to the fairly new but now quite zippy Austin A30.

An installation was also made in Jack's home. A listen and call time was set at 2230 hrs GMT. So wherever anybody's team was we could communicate, briefly in a coded manner. At least we would all be made aware of the basic goings-on. If a team had nothing to report they could listen. If they were in the field nobody would be concerned if no contact was made for a few days at least.

The little Austin ran a treat between Oxford and Cambridge. The dons were not happy with a girl moving all over campus asking questions and demanding time from some of their top chaps. Having a Frenchman with me was not too helpful either but Jack sorted a bit of paper out for us and we soon started to get the cooperation required from the boffins. Three separate physicists came up with the same answers; Erich's incredulous thoughts would seem to be getting confirmed.

The next stage was to look at all the manufacturing and government facilities involved with anything to do with nuclear stuff and uranium. Not a small task for what had been Bletchley Park, never mind us! I went to back to Jack and relayed the kind of scale this was heading towards and the mammoth task it could be, especially considering the possible timescales.

He looked at me and grinned, then said, "I have ten men and women who were in the service. They are all under my command and are awaiting your instruction!"

I answered with something rather out

of character, such as, "I could kiss you!" I smiled and said their instructions would be with him in the morning. They were in his office without his staff knowing by 0328 hrs. That way he would know we needed this to be kept well under wraps. The instructions were individualised so no individual would know what we were looking for and for their own safety. Within a week or so their information was starting to build a pattern. Just the fact that we had picked specific things to look in to was making a difference.

During this time, rather than go out to Operation Emu Field at Emu Junction, where the Totem nuclear tests had taken place and the second was due shortly, we were able to persuade some of the upper hierarchy twits that they might have a leak. That way the British Military could go in with the Australians and have a look around. I was then able to go to Australia and go in as a secretary and observe interviews during the day, then, shall we say, 'review' the complex by night. Most things were stopped for the weekend and that was the time Berty and I tested the facilities. To cut things short: we found that every measuring device had been tampered with or at least recalibrated to read on the heavy side. They all read over weight by the same amount. Easy to miss and easy to hide if you had a man or two on the inside. Who was dirty, I did not care; that was for security there. I had the damning information and I now needed to prove to myself the route out for the stolen uranium.

By road, overland in the area now

known as Maralinga, to the northeast of the test zone, there had been no dispersal of a radioactive cloud that later contaminated all the land up there. Who knows how many years it will be before it is safe up there again?

Looking at the possibilities of using a launch to catch up with a freighter, we could see that there were dozens of launch-friendly sites that could have been used in the timescales we had worked out, from our blackboard days. Then you could have flown and dropped a package next to the pickup vessel. The scope was too great and I needed to keep that ball rolling. I had Jack pull a few more strings; it was arranged that new measuring devices would be shipped into the test site's works and laboratories. Then security would be rescheduled and nobody, including the cleaners, would be allowed off-base until tests were complete. One bottle corked!

In the meantime the two boys in Ghana were having all sorts of fun. The heat and damp from the rainy season meant they were suffering; trying to lay low when you're not used to that kind of thing is tough - especially once the local wildlife realises you are the tender type, if you know what I mean. The garbled stuff that did come through on the longwave radio sets was: "We are coming home. Men missing and I have seen her again. It's nasty!"

There was no point in going to Nevada knowing what we had found in Australia. Beetle's boys could head that up now we knew to a degree what was possibly happening. They could also tidy their end up

and do as was being done in Australia.
Close the ruddy loopholes.

Erich and Stuart turned up back at the base
and were full of excitement, bounce, energy
and all that stuff. It transpired they had seen
a woman, small and beautiful, coming down
the gangplank of the freighter. They feared
that she was the lady that had been
described to us all by Christophe in the
catacombs in Paris, in 1945. She had gone
to the airport and flown to the UK. They had
followed as hard as they could. If we could
confirm that she was who they thought, and
things linked, then we may, just may, have
had the first real break in the case. This
beautiful woman had been a private
contractor to the SD and Gestapo during
World War II, based in Paris and doing her

stuff from Avenue Foche as the expert questioner and interrogator for those suspected of being allied spies who had been caught.

What Erich had actually said over the wireless set from Ghana was, 'Nazi.'

If she linked up with anything else that could be involved with the SR case then three dots can prove a line is straight and this would be the clincher. We would be in and on for the run home!

The four of us went into search patterns across London. Jack drew back his ten people and we were all off, looking for this little lady. She could have been anywhere in the UK. That is, if she was actually still in the UK. After several days she was spotted, followed and images were taken of her. These were cross-referenced with drawings made of her by survivors of her 'little chats' at Avenue Foche, in Paris - the few who had survived. Those who had still been breathing after being in concentration camps.

The artist impressions were all similar but not as good as an image stolen through a camera lens and seared onto film. Although the artist impressions were all just a tad different, the descriptions were so close that they had to be the same person. That image we now matched up with descriptions of stature, height, weight and facial features. It all seemed to match. My worry was, we were all on to the same thing; it's not often you get thrown an easy catch. We had little else so it had to be followed up: three shifts of three people on her, twenty-four hours a day, following her to *every shop; every café; every restaurant and every meeting. She ordered made to measure clothing of fashion at the best fashion houses. My thoughts (and those of a few of the girls that Jack had provided) were: if you have the money and can travel, why the blazes are you buying that kind of stuff here? Surely Paris was the correct place for the best fashion designers and incredibly beautiful jewellery?*

The images we now had were sent to Paris and the SDECE of the French Intelligence Agency was to inspect their files, as was the Israeli's. They came back with the same thing: wanted for questioning for suspected criminal acts during war and working with or for the Nazis. So yes, we had fallen onto a bit of luck; it had to be followed from a distance in the hope that it would lead us to the next option or step.

We left the ten to follow up and looked over their reports daily while trying to piece it all together. To date we had a confusing mixture of things to focus on and place into an order that looked like they might fit. It all needed to come together and start to build towards a logical goal.

So we had: Liberty ships. Smuggling? Gentlemen from Ghana being taken on to a vessel but never returning home. Uranium going missing. Modernised propulsion plants being exchanged on the Liberty ships for no economical reason. The extra hold in the engine room and the highly machined base of something on a bogie in that room.

Time to review the images from Brest again. There was nothing to be gained from *anything else. We knew what had gone missing and how. How deep the infiltration into the nuclear test sites was, was not our concern; the locals could sort that out in each country. We needed to understand* why *the thefts had taken place and what the intention was. Then maybe we could work out* how - *and stop it.*

One of the ten arrived with that day's reports. Her name was Charlotte - a stockily built girl with dark, unfashionably short hair. She was French, and it transpired that she had been in the Resistance in northern France. She had been heavily involved before D-Day in lighting up targets for the RAF.

By chance she saw one of the images on the screen that we were looking at and shouted out, "Bastards!" She lifted her arm and pointed to a section of the mounting plate being shown on the white screen board in front of us. They all spun to look at her as I took that day's file from her.

Almost in unison we asked the same question: "What?" Charlotte moved forward quite slowly and almost nervously, until she came close to the image showing. She pointed a finger at one small part of it. "There. I know what this could be!"

I asked her to take a seat and relax and asked one of the boys to make a cup of tea. After taking her raincoat off, Charlotte sat. She was wearing brogues in brown leather; green socks to her knees and a brown, woollen pleated skirt; a blouse under a round neck pullover, and no makeup. Her face was calm but white with shock - or fear.

At the time I was not sure which it could be. Once the tea arrived, we started to understand a few things a little better.

She had been with a local Resistance unit between Saint-Omer and Béthune. They had not been able to help with actions against the V1 flying bombs or the V2 rockets used against England. They had done their best at sabotage but were too weak and under armed to make a difference. She had, however, got into a work party for the Nazis when they had built the big bunker in that area. It had been dug down maybe one hundred and twenty feet. The way she described it, reinforced concrete many, many feet thick had been placed over the top to make it bombproof. It was probably more than six hundred feet long and not much less in width. Many rooms, offices and living quarters had been built in and massive areas for shells of immense size. Although the image on the screen was massively enlarged, she knew what it was. She had recognized a marking. Her actual shout, in astonishment, had been, "Bastard! That rose, it still lives!"

We all looked closely at the image and could now make out a very small symbol on the unit. Whoever had made this thing was proud of their workmanship. It was machined into the steel: the proper open head of a rose flower. The whole thing can only have been an inch in size.

Charlotte had been involved right up to the bombing of this emplacement, she and the men she worked with getting information out and back to the Allies. Nobody had believed the theory was possible, but the Nazis had built it all the same. It was a *multi-barreled Accelerator gun. Once the Allies began to understand how far advanced the Nazis were with this kind of technology, there was an all-out effort to destroy the facility. Several Lancasters were sent over with Barnes Wallis earthquake bombs.*

With British Special Forces and the Resistance, the RAF was able to make two or three direct hits. The establishment was flattened or sunk back into the hole that had been dug out to hide it in, and it was destroyed. It was finished off by ground personnel going in and finalising the job. It was a mess and not too pretty by her accounts. She had never been allowed to see the weaponry until this point. What she did say, was that the steelwork that was still visible had that emblem on. The tubes had been semi-upright and each one had small extensions sticking out; each small tube was angled up to one end. If they had been longer, the installation would have resembled a Christmas tree.

We all looked at each other and I took a seat, sitting down with a thump. We were ashen white. It was starting to come together. Three things linking up like this was no coincidence. A sitting stool that has only one leg is not stable. With two legs it is the same, but with three legs placed correctly, it is stable, sturdy and safe.

These guns could have flattened London in two days. They were designed to throw projectiles up into the stratosphere before they started to fall back down to earth. The range was estimated to be one hundred and fifty miles. The first explosion was to start at the base of the gun; then as the projectile moved up the barrel, a myriad of explosions was to go off in a specific fast sequence behind the projectile, continuously accelerating the ordnance ever faster up through the barrel until it leaped forth into the open, on its way to the targeted area. There could be no defence against such projectiles. The whole thing was horrific, once understood.

So it was possible that we had Accelerator cannons on vessels that were mobile and at sea; possible nuclear warheads that could be launched to anywhere from vessels that were almost impossible to track. Unless a warning was given, there was no way of knowing what the target was, or where the targets could be, *except they would need to be within roughly a one hundred and forty mile range of navigable waterways to ships of that size.*

We needed to trace the rose; whoever had made the units had survived the war well, maintaining its workforce, machinery and knowledge. We also needed to follow this woman and hope that she would lead us to the head of the organisation. Whatever they were up to, it was death to possibly millions and a living hell for many more. The world economy would be changed forever.

Then it struck me: they wanted control of the oil fields! This would mean government collapse and control of global economic resources. It was bloody well World War II all over again - but being fought out by stealth. The Nazi Third Reich just would not lie down and sodding well die.

I asked Charlotte to leave and voiced my thoughts to the boys. It was agreed: we were all in, we would stop it.

Once and for all time, or die trying.

Chapter 16: Chasing the Rose

Leaving the team to follow the pretty lady and chase down any and every lead that could be developed, I headed north. Peter Blyth had been in the machining business since university and he knew all there was to know about it He must know who had access to the correct quality of steel since the war, or, for that matter, during and before. He should know what companies since the war had a workforce left that had the skills to do such work. If he didn't, he might just know who did. Either way it was an opportunity to get an outsider's point of view. He would know of all the difficulties, and between us we could narrow the field down before actively going out and getting busy. The fewer offices and safes; the less security we would have to go through to find out what we needed to know, the better for us. Being in control of the game mattered immensely. The more that things could be narrowed down, the faster we would achieve results and get this sorted out.

I arrived with no notice at Gran's; she was over the moon to see me, and that was just fine. That lady could read me like a book.

She gave me a hug, looked into my eyes and said, "I can see it's work. Do what you need to do and let me know when you're leaving. I'm here to listen if you need me." I hugged her and went to bed.

The next morning I headed straight to Middlesbrough and to Blyth & Partners, entering by the office entrance. I got past reception and to Peter's secretary quite

quickly. Peter's secretary, on the other hand,
was a completely different kettle of fish. She
was beautifully slim at five feet ten inches -
plus her heels. She wore a tweed, pleated
red and green tartan business skirt, dressed
with a large kilt pin and topped with a
patent leather black belt. Over her elegant,
slender waist and covering her ample
breasts was a well-pressed, white cotton
blouse with a large collar. Over that was
fantastically well-fitted jacket that
emphasised this stunning figure. Her thick,
slightly wavy hair hung down loosely over
her shoulders. It was not the fashionable
way to have your hair, but she did look
good. Her face was slightly tanned and a
classic oval in shape. She was perfectly
proportioned to the broad shoulders. Her
eyes were a lively bright green, with strong,

clearly defined eyebrows. They missed nothing. Her nose was slender and her lips were full. Not too many men were going to get their own way with her but I can guarantee many must have tried. She spoke with a Berkshire accent and was obviously well-educated. I was just wondering where Peter had found this one when she looked up at me and asked who I was and what I wanted. We had not met on my first visit; I can't remember why but I knew we had not. She introduced herself as JJ McCloud, and I got to see the most perfect white teeth I had ever seen. I told her who I was and that I needed to see Peter. She wanted to know what it was about and I stalled and then said it was personal.

I was informed that Peter was away in the south on business but would be in the next day. If I was to return tomorrow at ten thirty am, it would be possible to see him during the coffee break; he was a very busy man and so on. Disappointed, I left.

The next morning, as I strode towards her, she rose from her desk to reveal her true elegance. She was the sort of creature you expected to see modelling in the magazines or at least working for some of the big city boys. How Peter had got hold of this one was beyond me! She shook my hand and took me straight through to Peter's office. He stood up from his big leather chair and smiled broadly then came round the desk and gave me the biggest bear hug I had received for ages. We went through the usual pleasantries before getting down to business.

During the early part of the

conversation I asked where the hell had that blond bombshell appeared from and how did he keep her on the payroll? He explained that one of his best engineers was Brian Kuzman, who ran the specialist project workshop. She was involved with him and they lived together. That particular workshop was where they really made the money for the business on government projects and jobs. Kuzman had arrived a year or two before the war and was invaluable to the business. He commanded the workshop brilliantly, solving problems and ironing them out to keep production on schedule during the war effort. He had a habit of organising and had a lot of his own engineers and turners, who never gave any trouble. Most of them were from Latvia and Lithuania as was he, escaping from the probability of what had actually happened before and then during the war. They had been exempt from fighting due to their highly valued skills and it had all worked well.

Peter still had no real idea of what I was there for. I mentioned that I presumed he must have signed the Official Secrets Act as he had such contracts. He told me that he had and so had all the workers in that particular workshop. It made me think a little but that was perfectly normal as far as I was concerned. I told him that I needed to pick his brains and run a few photographs by him; that I was looking for an organisation that would be able to carry out a certain kind of work - probably in Europe but not necessarily - and that any help at this point would be greatly appreciated. As I

*went through these pictures he looked up at
me and asked where I had acquired the
images from. I told him I could not tell him
but it was extremely important to find out
what I needed to know.*

*He looked at me with a question in
his eye again and said, "Well Sweetheart,
you have come to the right place. That's my
Yorkshire rose on the steel. We make those
pipes and bogies for the British
Government. Why on earth would you have
a picture of this?"*

*I stood up and walked slowly around
his desk. As I did so, I pulled my tyre pump
out of the side of my motorcycle boot. Peter
turned in his chair to face me and I placed
the end of the tyre inflator against his chest,
placing a little pressure on him through the
device. He looked at me and then down at*

the pump, wondering what I was doing. He asked what this was all about.

I said to him very slowly and clearly, "Either you're a traitor or you think I am a fool - or maybe you're a bloody idiot. I want to know: who in the government gave you your contracts? Where are the copy contracts? How have you been paid? Where are the units sent when built and when is your next shipment going out? Oh yes - and what is it you think you've have been making?"

He told me in a confident voice that they had shipped thirty nine units, thirty six during the war. They had all gone to the local port and been shipped to Ireland. Where the units were shipped to from there he did not know. The devices were very special and he thought they were going to be added to and used in the oil production industry. After that he could not tell me as he had signed the Official Secrets Act. I pushed the end of the pump a little harder into his chest and advised him that I needed a bit more than that.

He looked at me and shrugged, then repeated, "I can't tell you; they'll hang me if I do!" I could see we could dance around like this all day and was not prepared for it. I lowered the end of the pump down to below his belt towards his manhood, then passed on down and pushed it into the plush leather just in front of his crotch. Peter just looked at me, wondering what I was doing. Then with a gentle thrust, I pushed the pump a little deeper into the chair. As I did so, a small spring catch was released; several rubber rings and flaps yielded, just after a charge had been struck by a pin hammer held within the handle of the pump. It made a dull noise like a little thud and the pump kicked back slightly. All this happened in a few milliseconds. As a result, a one-inch hole appeared in his chair between his legs and a five inch hole appeared on the underside of his chair. Before he had a chance to look up I had a pistol to his shiny head with the hammer drawn back.

"Peter darling, I need some answers to those questions. Please understand that if you have been working for the other team, you will die in the next few minutes! Do you understand?" He nodded as sweat began to bead on his face and forehead. His hands had moved to protect his crotch and he had looked down with his steely blue eyes. He raised his head to face me; I could see in his *demeanour, face and eyes he was paying full attention to me now. I carried on: "So tell me, other than feeling happy you still have your tackle, how did your company get involved with producing accelerating guns?"*

He retorted, "Accelerator what?"

"Guns, Peter. Accelerator guns!"

"Don't be stupid! We don't do that kind of thing - we machine specialist steels to the drawings and, in this case, for the British Government. None of it has ever been remotely military."

"I need to see your contracts. I need to know who you deal with in the Civil Service."

"I told you last time I saw you!"

"You told me what last time we met?"

"Oxford Bob, the guy I told you about. He liaised and organised the contracts then brought the drawings and plans here. He also organised our payment. He is due here in a week or two to check over the last two units that are being finished now."

I walked back around the desk and sat down in a chair, still pointing my pistol toward him. JJ was knocking on the door, wanting to know if anything was wrong. Peter called her in and told her he had dropped a file and he was sorry if she had been alarmed. I kept my pistol still pointed at him out of her line of sight. He knew it, and was holding up well. His eyes were not that of a conspirator but those of an innocent man. Was he an idiot or had the wool really been pulled over his eyes? Was he that crafty - or stupid?

"You mentioned this bloody Oxford Bob. Who the hell is he?"

"His correct name is Stephen Robinson. You can never get hold of him, but that's how the Civil Service works. When they want you they are all over you. He seems to get on well with JJ but what man is not going to fall over for her? He often has meetings with Kuzman and takes him out for lunch. I have always assumed the meetings are on technical issues but they could also be about JJ. Kuzman is not a jealous man, if you know what I mean."

"OK Peter. I am beginning to see a reason, possibly, to allow you to stay alive for now. I need to explain a few things to you and hope you understand it all. Just nod if you're willing." *He did so while still*

sweating and looking a little pale. I went through our story so far.

He looked at me and said, "I really can't confirm anything here. You do not know what he looks like so it may or may not be the same man. Yes, the units are mine but I can't see anyone wanting to do what you say you think they might! The only thing that remotely fits is the woman who is often with him, Ciao Bella: she's small, stunning and moves with a style and assurance that - well; you just do not see anywhere. Except for JJ and yourself, of course."

"OK Peter; as I have known you forever, I am going to give you the benefit of the doubt. There are some things that you are going to do for me. You are going to keep your mouth shut - but you are going to help me. I need the following: a tour of the specialist machining area of the factory, once all the staff members have gone home. To save time and effort, I want copies of the blueprints of everything else, whether you think it may be of interest or not. I need skeleton keys for all the buildings, safes and anything else that may get locked up. I want Kuzman and this JJ girl's home addresses. You talk to anyone and it will be the last words you ever say. I hope trusting you until I dig this out is the correct thing to do. You could go sick for a week if you choose. I will be off to London this afternoon and back tomorrow. If you want or are willing to help then that is fine. Meet me in the Wheat tomorrow evening at eight. Berty will be with me. I will have decided by then how things are going to be dealt with."

I turned to leave and Peter said,

"Everything you need will be with me at the Wheat. If I have been duped then I want to know about it and help. If you're wrong, I will want to kick your arse as if it were a rugby conversion!"

I carried on walking towards the door of his office, raised my right arm and retorted with, "If I'm wrong darling, you can lose your bloody foot up there!" and left.

The train from Darlington was uneventful and I met up with the lads in London. It was all starting to come together in my mind; a lot of supposition and there were many things that were a guess, but I had a strong feeling of satisfaction that I was on the right scent.

Berty and I left London the next morning on

the early train, leaving Erich and Stuart to head the team following the woman now known to be Ciao Bella as closely as possible.

We met Peter and had a good dinner as he handed over all I had requested. Peter left to go home and the two of us went back to Gran's cottage. Together we went over the blueprints of the Accelerator and were able to confirm that even though it was only through luck, it was what we had seen in Brest. We now needed to get into Peter's workshops and offices for a little more snooping. If Peter was not the villain then somebody else was. We were going to have to go through Kuzman and JJ's personal desks and then through their private dwellings to clear them. If it was not them, we needed to know who. Either way, there had to be an inside person or connection to SR. It was just a case of breaking into every building that was connected and going through any paperwork we could find.

The next night we left the cottage around ten and headed into Middlesbrough. Leaving the Vincent at the railway station, we headed over the border to Blyth & Partners' buildings. I had no idea but there were an uncanny number of ladies of the night around and a number of inebriated men wanting to help them earn a living. One chap actually offered Berty and me a good time. Unhappily for him, he was still laid out where I left him a few hours later as we passed by.

The skeleton keys worked a treat and saved us many minutes looking for the best entry points. Our first place to look was in the special workshop. Yes: the units at the end of production were the same as the one we had seen in Brest. These things were massive. The French girl who had identified the marking on the Accelerator guns in Saint-Omer had seen it correctly. It was the place we had needed to be. But now we had found the manufacturer we needed to know how the operation was working.

Kuzman's office was the next place to go through. We had no keys for his desk but the locks were easily picked and we went through all his paperwork. There was nothing that jumped out at us until Berty spotted the oddest thing: in this workshop there was not one English name. Every employee was from outside the UK - Latvian or Lithuanian by the first part of the surname. Pretty much all just had 'man' at the end. The Christian names were all basic, short English. There was handwriting on some of the documents but it was a little too dark working with torchlight to read. Between us we photographed what we could to look at a later date.

The next day it was to Kuzman's home - a small, discreet cottage in Great Ayton, just opposite the river Esk which runs through the centre of the village. In the property there were no family pictures and not much to go by. JJ obviously lived there too and the place was a bloody mess. Still; we went through every damned thing. There was nothing: no unpaid bills, not even an old letter lying around.   It was too clean when it came to condemning evidence. So we were back to the factory that night, avoiding the ladies of the night and *everybody else.*

JJ's desk was a different matter. In her desk, we made discoveries which helped a few things start to fall into place. There were private communications with Robinson but they were sordid and very private; not really the sort of thing we were looking for. They were also not the kind of thing you would keep at work unless your partner knew nothing about it! There were a few expensive trinkets that you couldn't buy on her kind of salary. That was something to come back to, after a talk with Peter. It was possible he was involved with the woman in a personal manner too! She was stunning and obviously not a shy girl!

For me, the letters were not too interesting but Bert really wanted to take his time reading them. If it stimulated some memories from the past and changed our future a bit I was not going to argue. We needed to go back through all the workers' records and try and find a link. That would have to be done with the two of us working together, as going through personnel lockers would be laborious, and probably painstakingly boring!

I took a little time to wander around the offices and have a good snoop. The filing cabinets revealed little and it seemed Peter took a lot of information regarding his team on trust, which is great until you get involved with a few rum ones. I've never been one for accounts books but as I was in, according to the sign on the door, the office of 'Mr. Norman Brown, Head of Accounts', I had a finger through his files. Oh what a tangled web some can weave! There were *two sets of books: one with Peter's signing off and one more than he might know about! I took images with the camera of a few pages from each of the accounts books, pulled Bert out and left the offices as we had found them.*

That night I slept well, knowing that at least the probability was that Peter was straight. Naïve, possibly, but straight. Once the images were developed, I would be able, after talking with an accountant, to trust the bit of knowledge I had.

The next move was to go through Mr. Brown's activities and life style. I didn't want to meet him or challenge him until I had a bit more information to lean on. So while the images were being developed, we took a look at Mr. Brown's home from the outside and watched him for a day or two. It happened now to be the weekend; these images would not be developed until the Monday, so what the hell!

Mr. Brown turned out to be a tall, thin, greying man. 'Wet' is how I would describe this bookworm. Collarless shirt; long sleeves and a waistcoat; polished shoes and about as much life in him as a battered sprat! Probably never lifted anything heavier than a matchstick, and then it would only have been a spent one. His home was in Acklam: a well-to-do area of Middlesbrough, out of the smoke and at that time fairly rural still. It was the posh people's belt, as it were, where solicitors and business owners resided. Unless he was a shareholder or partner in Blyth & Partners, he was doing things way over his head. We had been outside his property since six that morning, waiting for something to happen. His wife, or partner, was up at that time cleaning, exercising and lala-ing around the house. Then at about eight, she closed the curtains. God knows what she was doing then.

He, the lanky, insipid twerp, came out of the house at about the same time. A cab appeared and he was off in it to Middlesbrough railway station. He had a briefcase as if going to work, but he obviously was not. We followed from a distance in the A30, until we reached the station. Bert went into the station, while I waited in the car parking area. Bert came out and said we needed to beat the train to Darlington, home of the railway. Brown had acquired tickets with a next-day return to

King's Cross. The train he was heading for now was the 10:01 from Darlington, stopping at Yarm, Thirsk, York, Doncaster, Peterborough and King's Cross. It would arrive at King's Cross around 5.10 pm. Brown may have seen me with Peter, although we had not been introduced. The move was to get Bert on the London train to study him and for me to get to London before the train and have the team ready to follow discretely.

Bert was on the smoking giant at Yarm. I raced to Bagby, near Thirsk - a private little club strip that I had a few friends at, from before the war. As I arrived, one or two chaps recognised me and we all did a bit of shoulder slapping - as you do!

The long and the short of it was: I blagged an aeroplane and was off before the offer was retracted. It was a low-winged thing and was as close to flat out as I dared. One hundred and thirty knots was about all it trimmed out at. Fortunately I had a slight tail-wind most of the way which dropped off near Peterborough. It was a little smoggy over the city but at only five hundred feet you can still pick out some landmarks through it. Soon I was past and located good old 'Biggy.' Joining the circuit, I looked to see if there was any traffic. There seemed to be none and as I had no wireless set in the little lady, I just went straight down the throat of the runway as quickly as possible.

Once the kite was stopped, I cut the fuel and flipped the 'Mags' off, stopping the fan from turning anymore. RAF Engineers ran out towards me, with a few military personnel who were going to try to detain me for landing on a military base. I alighted enthusiastically from the little aircraft and started to move with all haste towards the oncoming men, dropping two of the buggers on my way to the CO's office. Once there, I knocked on the door and introduced myself. I handed my I.D. over and asked him to call Jack. He did so and his face changed from that sweaty red of temper to the whiteness of subservience. His guys got me into London pdq and I was with my team with forty minutes to spare. Briefing was sharp; then we were on the move. Once the platform was located we took our places. We watched.

Then I felt that funny feeling of being in the right place at the right time. There, coming onto the platform, was a petite, hip-swinging, beautiful woman, being watched (badly, I might say) by two of the ten we had on loan. It was her. For the first time, I was actually seeing the bitch - that evil little bitch - who had destroyed so many lives; who had tortured my uncle, Christophe and so many others.

It was all I could do not to race forward and tear her head off, but Erich held me back and calmly said into my ear in a soothing way, "There is a time and place for that. Now we have a job. She is just one of the locks we have to pick to get in. Once the job is complete, you can do as you please with her, but now it is vital we gather all we need to fulfil your promise to Jack, your uncle and your four faithful followers. For that matter to the known world, you swore in Poland when we witnessed the nightmare of 'Darkness and fog' and those Nazi bastards!"

I saw Bert alight from the carriage just as the great steam engine came to a halt and clouds of white steam plumed from her pistons. Then for a moment I could see nothing until Bert appeared again through the dissipating cloud. He was followed, unintentionally by Mr. Brown who, as soon as he saw her, headed for that evil little woman and he gave her a lover's hug. I knew then we were in; this would lead us to the endgame!

I dispersed my troops, as it were, and we started to run a professional tailing routine. The pair took us across London from King's Cross over to Harrods, where some purchases were made. Then on to Soho and into a few clubs - seedy is not the word! - even some of the lads were a little surprised at the activities going on inside

*these unpleasant places. The two of then
entered a blinking massage parlour and I
began to get a little more than perturbed by
their meandering through the city. As far as
I was concerned, they had no idea as to who
I was - or Erich (Brown may have seen
Bert).   So Erich and I went into the
establishment and basically said, "Whatever
is good enough for those two is good enough
for us!"*

*Next thing I knew, we were stripped
naked and given covering towels. The four
of us – Mr. Brown, Ciao Bella, Erich and I -
were given an enthusiastic massage in a
room with six tables lined up side by side.
The persons giving the massage, as far as I
was concerned, really just attacked me!
What the others thought I do not know. I do
have to say I have had much, much better,*

but then that was in a slightly more pleasant area and time!

Once the rubbing had ceased, we were ushered into a sauna room. Nazi Woman took a bunk on the left hand side of the room and just let her towels drape around her. I was not going to do the same but took the bunk to the opposite side and sat with my towels covering my femininity. Erich sat by my side and kept his manhood covered too. Mr. Brown however - all six feet two inches of the skinny bugger - dropped his towel right in front of my face, looked me in the eye and grinned as bullies do! He then gestured that he intended to get on the bunk above my head. As he stretched and stepped up over my head, I got an eyeful of the dangly bits as well as the exit area. It was not pleasant and it took all my inner strength not to strangle it - or him. I began to seethe and sweat as did Erich. Erich may have been in a sauna before but it was a first for me. Every time she poured water on the hot stones I swore to myself and nearly fainted. Nobody talked and eventually a man dressed in white (as were the masseurs) told us that time was up; to get out and go to the quench pool. Those Swedes must be crazy! The water was freezing and was likely to give you a heart attack. I laughed to myself when Brown came out of the pool, his towel now sharply up against his shrunken tackle. Through that entire ordeal we had learned nothing, except that the Swedish are utterly mad.

Any following was now going to have to be through a third party as Erich and I could not be seen so close to the quarry again. So Stuart and one other took over the close surveillance stuff and Bert and I hung back, then settled back at headquarters to see how things unfolded. The two under the team's watchful eye, after a few more shops, ended up at the Savoy. There they retired to a pre-booked room.

Later that evening - around eight - they came down through reception and into the dining room for dinner. With them for dinner was a smooth, well-tanned chap, dark haired with round, rimmed tortoiseshell glasses. Stuart noted that if any of the waitresses passed him close enough a hand went out and pinched them on the bottom. Every woman seemed to be stripped of their dignity, assessed and reassessed in his mind and through those brown, piercing eyes.

By this time Stuart had called in from

the foyer payphone to us. He had been able to wangle a table close to the three individuals of interest. It had cost him all he had, as well as his Omega Pilot's watch given to him by one of the pilots we had helped during that desperate war. He needed money to pay for the dinner once it had been consumed; they needed to look at ease and give the air that money was never a concern. That kind of finance was not to hand and we were in the poop, as it were.

In the end I called Jack, who was able by telephone to get a few chums in to save the day, dropping in enough cash so that the maître d'hôtel was able to say to my boy, "Sir, You have been recognised by the manager. Your dinner, wine of your choice and your room is on the house. As our guest, it is the least we can do for the honour of having you within our establishment. You will of course accept our hospitality?"

Stuart took it on the chin and started to reply with, "Thank you, it is appreciated but my partner and I would prefer to remain incognito."

"You are sir, and your visit here will remain undisclosed!"

"Then I thank you; it will make no difference as to our future but our intention is not to stay overnight. Our luggage and place of residence for this evening is just along the way."

"Sir, it would be our pleasure to recover your transit baggage from your present residence and return it here to the suite of your choice"

Stuart replied, "As you wish. Here is the address for the luggage. Thank you!"

He then ordered the wine for the evening meal and the maître d' sauntered off to his duties.

At this point the new man who had joined Mr. Brown and Miss Bella for dinner leant across and piped up in a brash American accent, "Hey Irish! You must have some business going on in this town to get that kind of service from these boys. Can I buy you a drink in the bar a little later? I like a man with style, and you seem to have more style in your wallet than most. I have to book a month in advance to get what I want here - you get it without asking. I think I would like to know how to get myself some of that kind of recognition!"

Stuart had no choice but to engage in the conversation and offer to have a drink in the bar, after a dinner had been consumed *in a relaxed, easy-going fashion.*

The bar was plush and made out of oak, highly polished and darkened with age. A brightly polished foot rail ran the length of it, just below the panelling. The top of the bar was clean and beautifully cared for. A few polished brass drink draining trays were placed in front of the beer pumps. The wall behind the bar was mirrored with three layers of shelves, stacked with every form of alcohol beverage you could imagine. We had not had time to get others in with microphones to record anything and so would have to rely on Stuart and his partner's version of events. However, we were able to get a photographer in with a press badge. He was able to get several shots of Stuart for a paper he claimed to be with, saying he recognised Stuart. The shots were all just off-target, giving us images of Brown, Bella and this new guy.

The new guy never took his eye off the young ladies, nudging them whenever he could. Other than his name, he had given Stuart nothing that could be searched for or researched. That was not of concern when I debriefed him. What was of concern was making sure the team of ten could keep tabs on the three of them while we verified a few things.

First thing was to develop the negatives and get Jack to have them moved around a few places using his contacts, primarily the witnesses at the Nuremberg trials as well as any other survivors of the Holocaust. I needed to tie a few ideas up and get some history on this man. Did he *have a criminal record? Where had he come from and why was he meeting these two?*

After a little checking and the handing over of money, we were able to learn that Bella and the other guy were staying in this particular hotel for three days before leaving.

Brown left the hotel and scampered across town to catch the 15:45 from King's Cross back up to Darlington, leaving the other two. They had been out most of the day while the team watched and Berty and I went through their adjoining rooms slowly and carefully. We had time to place a few microphones and run the cables through vents into the next room, where we were to set up a listening post. There was nothing incriminating in the rooms; about all we got was his shaving gear (and a few other things that did happen to have the initials SR on them). His passport, held in the hotel's safe, also revealed that he was an American citizen by the name of Stephen Robinson. The passport was fairly new but had a fair few stamps in it from travelling around the world. He had travelled to at least thirty different countries in the past two years. You don't do that unless you have an immense income or you are unbelievably wealthy. The visits to countries definitely did not tie in with any form of holiday circuit. Her passport was similar and date stamps in the passport showed that the two of them had crossed paths thirteen times at least during those two years. Later, studying the images of the passports, we were able to link several things but we still had no concrete evidence of anything.

I left the team following them, and headed north following Brown; he had a briefcase that had something in it and I wanted to know what. I was on the same train just a carriage away, keeping an eye out at all the stops for his departure.

Thirty-six hours later I was going through Brown's office and files. Yes, there were two sets of books and he was stealing from the business - but there had to be more to it all.

The next day I waited for Mrs. Brown to leave her home to go for some shopping or her hair to be done or whatever in the Acklam area. I was in and out in twenty minutes, leaving no signs of entry, exit or of anything being moved in the house. It was bloody well there and I still nearly missed it - what a fool. There were two images of Mr. and Mrs. Brown and one included Mr. Robinson which was in itself innocent enough. However, on the back of the images within the frame were the dates the images were taken and where: one was 1934, in Berlin and the other was September, 1935, in Munich. Now that was incriminating evidence in my book. At least one of them was possibly German. I needed to talk to Peter and find out how long Brown had been with Blyth & Partners.

Not wanting to see Peter at work where walls may just have ears, I went to his home. It was the first time I had met Sue, his wife and his three children, Antonia, Anthony and Sybil. All four of them were a delight to spend time with over a cup of tea while I waited for the big man to return. When he did arrive through the door, his *smile and sense of love for his family shone through as he opened his arms and hugged Sue. The little people were all over him like a rash for attention, and each got their fair share. Then he noticed that I was sitting in the corner of the dimly lit lounge, the small windows in the old cottage blocking out most of the sunlight from this extraordinarily old and beautiful room.*

As Sue went to bring in a fresh brew and the children went outside to play again, Peter looked at me asked, "What have you found? Just tell me and I will deal with it!" In reply, I went through what we had witnessed in London, seen in Brown's office and found in Brown's house. Peter fell back in his chair hard and fast. Tiny particles of matter plumed up in the sunlight from the cushions of the chair, cascading through the light and refracting it all over the room.

His eyes darkened and he looked up at me. "In the back of my mind I suppose I always wondered how such well-paid government contracts had made their way to us. I hoped it was the old school tie thing and we are just dashed good at what we do."

"Oh Peter," I replied. "That is the problem. Someone at university probably assessed you and the family business well before the war. Once your talents and the business were verified as possibly useful with specialist skills, it was then just a case of how to access your workforce. I need to verify and go through vetting all of Kuzman's men, but it is now occurring to me that they had the sense to escape from the Nazis well before the war and find work *where their abilities could be put to some advantage against their enemy. It is just very sad that all that effort, in the end, may have been going to the Nazi war machine anyway. What a buggered up world this can be; little changes! We were making munitions in the northwest, shipping to Northern Ireland, where the goods were exported to Germany, only then to be fired at our own men in the trenches during the 'Great War'."*

"I need to know, Peter," I said, "but I can see it in your eyes; you are not involved are you?"

Peter nodded as if to say, "No," while keeping a covering hand over his dangly bits inside his trousers. I think his memory was drawing him back to his office chair.

"OK then Peter; I am going to need

you to work with my team and myself. I will tell you what is at stake when it is all over. In the meantime, change nothing. I will be in contact as and when I need. My team and I will come and go but will not disturb anything until I have a plan. Once a plan is formulated and is in place, and every part of this jigsaw is where I need it to be, we will act. Then you will know!"

We shook hands and I left his home after saying goodbye to his wife and children.

Chapter 17: Kuzman

Steve Robinson was now back in Brest to look at the final alterations to his three Liberty ships. Security had remained tight between his visits and the relevant alterations had all been made. The new high-performance diesel motor had been installed. The strengthening of deck plates had been completed and bulkheads placed around to allow concealment. The deck above had been altered appropriately to allow mounting of the equipment that was to be dispatched from Blyth & Partners shortly. Now there was only technical stuff left to do. His specialist smelting vessel would arrive soon. Its cargo would be the slaves from Ghana, who, on their way home with their riches, would sadly find a way overboard, to be consumed as fodder. These men and their families would never reap the rewards of their hard labour.

Robinson had remained fairly nomadic; his life was spent on the move. He had suites permanently rented in many of the best hotels for his personal use. Each one had all the facilities he required and they were usually within an hour of a sea port or aerodrome by car. All the staff at these hotels knew him well, not for tipping and not for being polite but for being the man always with a different woman. Some were beautiful and some were not, but it did mean he left the staff alone. He did have offices in Greece where his fleet were registered; he visited the offices of the company every month for several days.

Whatever Robinson's plan was it stayed in his head. Interpol looked; my team looked and the end result was twelve ships, all with possible armament. Three to be fitted out with the new units that were made by Peter and Kuzman, I assumed. It all kept coming back to putting all the parts of the puzzle together in the correct order without taking a leap of faith. Enriched-grade uranium 232 product missing from three explosion test sites, enough to make three reasonably sized bombs, and even bigger if they were to be made 'dirty', as it were. Vessels that were for no apparent reason very fast and two which had disappeared for a number of days without notice. High shareholdings in profitable oil fields around the world.

For all we looked and looked, we could not see his direct objective. There were only three things we could do. These were: sabotage the vessels and guns; observe and learn. That was it! With no known objective and no understanding of their plan, there was little we could do. It was all making my knickers itch. Firstly, we had to quiz Kuzman and then go through his men. Secondly, we needed to tackle JJ and see if she was in on whatever was going on. Somehow we needed an inside man. Kuzman was a wily old bugger. His spoken English was still with an accent, which in a tough shipyard town like Middlesbrough, throughout the war, must have been rough enough. To be paid well enough to live out in Great Ayton on the Green meant that Peter remunerated him well which could also cause issues. Thirdly: JJ lived with him and they had different surnames. That was *never going to go down well in pre or post-war England.*

He was a stout man with a long, untidy beard hanging well off his chin. His hair was combed and creamed back, making the upper half of his face looked anaemic. He wore a tweed jacket over a blue, wrinkled shirt with a tight collar. His tie was wool and went right up to the fastened top button. It turned out he was of Jewish extraction; not personally religious but it had been on his records. He had been in Germany as Mr. Hitler was wielding his way to power, He had seen what was going on and had just wanted out. When he had gone home, he had struggled to persuade people to leave their homes and run. He had tried Australia, New Zealand, American and Canada but could not afford the passage.

England, he knew, was going to be hard but
he came anyway.

He had tried to find work in all the
shipbuilding areas but no one had offered
him a job, until Mr. Blyth. Mr. Blyth was a
great man in Kuzman's eyes; he had seen
and recognized this. 'Brian' Kuzman's
training and skills soon allowed him to run
his own shop. He had been in contact with
his brothers at home and got some to come
and work here at Blyth & Partners. Some of
the men who were all young had brought
their girlfriends, and some had now settled
with local girls. They were all happy and
more importantly, still alive; that was all
that mattered.

The Boche; the Nazis; the Third
Reich had gone; the world was a safer and
better place. They had played their part,

building the best, machining the best for the British. They and he had not gone to fight; their war had been fought in the machine shops making what they believed nobody else could. He had never heard of their work being used but he assumed that what they had built was so devastating it would have been top secret and nobody would ever really know about it.

Chapter 18: Finding Oxford Bob

It took a while, but eventually the five of us came up with a plan to board one of the vessels and sabotage one of the units. Charles and Berty came up with the blinking idea. It was not insane but it meant on review that I needed to bring in an old friend - if we could find him. Erich and Stuart were sent off to secure information on which of the target vessels had been fitted with a unit and their voyage plans. This information was needed to help us acquire the correct tracking vessel for the kind of waters the vessel would be in.

It seemed that our points of entry were going to be one of two. Both were going to have to be at night when fewer crew members would be around. I needed Berty's deft touch and skills to cover the first method of access, and the second, which was just as dangerous, he could do with me. The second method of access to a vessel was not discussed at this particular time.

Erich and Stuart went on their way to find the information required, while Brian Kuzman was brought to us to discuss how to sabotage the actual units. He needed to understand that weight was an issue while trying to board a vessel. Sinking a vessel was easy but the result of that could be too great, and a danger to shipping and the world. We needed to neutralise this weapon without alerting the owner. Once Brian understood the implications, he slotted right into the team. Although he was a heavy metal engineer, he understood electronics as they were then, and how the units were to be fired: explosions set off in a sequence that would continuously accelerate the projectile up the barrel.

His solution was brilliant. Simple, but brilliant all the same. Basically we needed to alter the firing order of the individual charges. So instead of firing off the charges microseconds apart in a vertical direction pushing the projectile ever faster up the tube, he would, we assumed, cause the action to go the other way. We were dead wrong in this instance!

If it was done it might only cause damage to the loading breach, which could probably be repaired quickly depending how good the crew were. Kuzy, as we started to call him, wanted to split the tube or barrel, rendering it useless for all time. However, the sabotage had to be done in a way that meant it would only do its thing when they fired the actual terrible weapon.

He had seen two potential firing systems once, when he had met the 'British Intelligence' man now known to be Robinson. They had discussed some of the machining difficulties during and post-war (that meant the ballistics expert and Nazi had actually been coming over to Middlesbrough during the war - another mystery that needed to be sorted). One system was pretty much the same as used to run a car and create the sparks at the spark plug. High tension leads ran from the charges along the barrel back to a distributor. There were two distributors, each with eight leads coming from the barrel and one centre lead coming in from a coil. The coil created a continuous high voltage *to the distributor; a rotating arm and a rotor opened and closed a set of points. A rotating arm picked up the current and as it turned on its access, the tip of the arm would make contact with what was a connector to each lead. The lead then allowed the pulse of power to travel through it to the charge. It was to trigger each explosion in the sequence desired. Driving these units were gears that were all too difficult to get to in a hurry (I thought just some sand or grinding paste into the unit would have been enough or destroy the internals). Seemingly, they had spares for everything and the gears would only run for a few seconds in testing and the same for the firing sequence. The reliability of this set of gears that Brian had designed and machined were of a quality and standard that were his duty to the*

British war effort. As he said: better safe than sorry. Now he was sorry!

This solution was going to take three or four minutes and would need no equipment; we would just change the firing order of the leads at the distributor from 1-2-3-4 to 16. He wanted to fire them off 2-3-4 to 8 and simultaneously 16-15-14 down to 9. The imbalance of the firing and reverse order meant the explosion would be driven to the centre of the barrel and thus split the barrel and render it irreparable.

Possible system two was a little less easy for me to understand. This had fine wires running up and down the launch tube to fire each charge. The same sequence of events would need to happen but it would be controlled in a manner that was beyond me. Berty of course understood, but there was no way he could come on at least one of his proposed methods to attempt to access a vessel. We needed to conjure up what one would call an inside man. That man, if we could find him, needed to be not more than seven stones in weight; small, good with his hands and fast. The only little man that I knew of had been an instructor of mine when going through the SOE training. He was Sergeant Major Alex Dunn and was just the best official instructor I had ever had; a little small in stature but a damned big man in reality.

He always said to me, "Do your job from as far away as possible, i.e. with a rifle or bomb! If not, get inside and so close that your opponent cannot use their power, strength or weapons against you. Hit first, make it count and don't stop until it is over.

Then get out fast."

The best example I can recall was while I was in training for the SOE. It was at a dance a group of us went to, when we were actually given a weekend pass.

Five of us met at a venue. He was already there, making sure we were punctual His trilby was tilted jauntily to one side and down at the front a little. His short-cropped, strawberry blond hair was just too short to flicker in the extremely light breeze. He smiled at us as we arrived, showing his almost perfect, bright, white teeth with his broad, happy smile. He was close-shaven and you could see that he hardly had to shave, even though he must have been in his very late twenties. His nose had never been broken but had remained straight and narrow, with no flaring. His eyes were glassy bright with almost watery wetness over the iris. One was green and the other brown and it was this that had stopped him working abroad during the war in the field we were in; he was just too recognisable and memorable. Once seen never forgotten! He moved with a grace that embarrassed most women, light on his feet and silent when he needed to be. On the dance floor later saw that evening, I saw that he was just wizard. He wore a double-breasted, grey flannel suit jacket. Underneath was a white shirt with a blue and white polka dot tie; a matching hanky, pressed and folded, poked out of his left breast pocket. Pleated trousers with turn ups led down to a highly polished pair of brown brogues.

There were a lot of men and not too many ladies at the venue. Alex picked out one particular lady - you know the type: the professional who stands in front of a camera in various states of dress, usually selling something glamorous. This one Alex thought was just about right for him that evening. He did as he should and introduced himself and they had a dance or two together; she was obviously attached but he just did not care!

He returned to our group and said that he would not be returning to our billet that evening, as he had an engagement. I was impressed at his five feet two inches of confidence and attitude; his dancing was great, but the lady already seemed to have a partner, who also had a friend. He came over and whispered in my ear that he was nipping outside for two or three minutes and if this gentlemen and his friend followed could I and or one of our team follow him.

He went; they followed. We allowed the required time to elapse and then followed too. He had, in his wisdom, gone to urinate in a toilet cubicle. I think he put the seat of the toilet down and sat on it.

Then he waited for these guys to turn up and have a go. They did, bursting through the door after checking from under the door that it was he who occupied the cubical. The door burst open, the ferocity of their entrance stripping the lock away from the door post. As the two guys struggled to get their shoulders into the small space and have a go at Alex, he smiled. The two gentlemen looked at Alex in amazement and shock, expecting to see an easy target sitting on the loo with his trousers down. The intention was to warn the well-dressed man off for talking to one of the chaps' wives, and if need be knock seven bells out of him. What they in fact walked into was a fearless man who knew what he was doing.

Not realising that they had walked straight into his calculated little trap of hell, they saw him grin. Alex looked at the two big men. He gently shook his head from side to side, took a deep breath and looked around while still smiling. As they came in, they towered above him. He moved forward inside their personal space and started. His fists blurred in a series of hammer blows to the gentlemen's ribs. His arms moved like the pistons on a locomotive running flat out and the sound was as if a silenced machine gun was hurling its load as fast is its recoil would allow. His arms moved back and forth in four-inch jabs, each one making its mark on the target ribcage. The jabs were not *intended to break the ribs but to bruise them to a point where breathing was much, much more than a laboured effort. Then he went lower and started to bruise the internal organs until the two chaps seemed to liquefy in front of our eyes and melted down to the ground. He stopped as they dropped, knowing he had done enough, never even breaking sweat. He stepped back, stood and straightened his tie and suit jacket and stepped out over the two unconscious bodies, He looked up and smiled at us.*

Then placing his little hands together, he stretched his fingers out without cracking his knuckles and said to us all, "That's grand then; nothing broken." He lifted his head towards us as he walked over. I looked at him quizzically and he laughed, saying, "Sorry Sweetheart; what I meant was, none of their ribs are broken. Once found, they will be in hospital for a few days while the bruising settles. I hit no flasks or objects in their pockets so my hands are fine. Now for the lady; we'll be off and I will return to the training barracks 0800 hrs next Monday, which officially is my thirty-six hours off." As he walked back into the dance hall, he shouted, "Cheers!" to us and I began to understand what he meant by the phrase 'Inside, inside!'

Nothing ever fazed Alex Dunn; he was the man I needed for our proposed action. Jack was the man who could find him so he was asked to do so; then it would be up to me to persuade him to join the team.

Erich and Stuart were now following Mr.

Robinson - not with absolute ease, as he moved very frequently. Every few days they would be asking me for funds, staying in much less voluptuous accommodation than Mr. Robinson as they travelled around Europe by rail, including the Orient Express from Paris to Venice. The cheeky buggers lived it up on caviar and whatever wine Erich decided was the correct one for the day. I doubt the waiters had too much influence.

When I saw them next, at least they had had the decency to lose the weight they had put on. It reminded me that once, the privilege of this journey had been mine, when I was young with my father. I was young - too young to drink - and my simple tastes could not be trained to enjoy the salty Beluga caviar; to me it was just fish eggs *and horrible. I could see the divine and luxurious bar area and watch a few romantic couples dance and live the dream of the journey. Plush was not the word; it was as close to palatial as it could have been - although it just happened to be on wheels. It made me laugh though; soot still came in through the windows and no matter how much the poor porters, waiters and staff cleaned it was always there, making people look grubby and slightly blackened.*

More importantly, the lads' reports were coming in by telegram with postcards and letters following, providing us with more and more detail. The telephone calls were just about always for funds. The picture and pattern of this man's three-monthly routine was building: Teesside to the Rhine; up the Rhine and then across to

Paris to visit some friends, shall we say, and engage a lady for company for a week or more. Then on to Venice where she would be disengaged and sent back third-class to her place of work back in Paris.

On this particular visit to Venice, Szabados and Tovan Albero were playing in the Chess Championships. The match was drawn when a King's Indian attack was thwarted by an East Indian defence. Robinson and Miss Bella had tickets and watched the great chess minds clashing in competition. What it showed me was the following: Robinson was obviously, as we knew, an intelligent man, but he did admire planning and an overview of things. With this assumption in mind, I hoped that he still had little idea that we were on to him or his organisation, as he had not acted in a defensive manner at least.

He met up with Ciao Bella in Venice and they spent a day or two together in the best restaurants and hotels around the Grand Canal, discussing much which was unknown to us. Just as the boys were relaxing in this plush, expensive and beautiful historic part of the world, thinking this man was a doddle to follow, the two they were watching disappeared. It took them a whole day to understand what had happened and by then it was too late. The two of them had been in the hotel where the target and Miss Bella the fantastic décor and guests of this magnificent hotel as they entered and exited by Gondola. The food was exquisite and the service exquisite; fit for kings, was how it was described to me. Looking at the finances being consumed it must have been.

*It was bringing the Yorkshire out in me,
arranging for monies to go to the boys.*

*They had been looking through the
newspapers, while sitting close to the
water's edge so as not to be too noticeable.
At around 1000 hours, a vessel sailed
through the Grand Canal. Many of these
large cargo vessels, as well as ocean liners,
followed during the day. This had been the
pattern every day; actually the last
commercial cargo ship to use the Grand
Canal in Venice was as late as 1968. These
ships came pretty close to the front of the
hotels and other buildings and the lads were
discussing how tight it must be for the
captain and first mate and what pressure
they must be under. These vessels towered
above where they were sitting and were just
enormous. This particular vessel had come*

so close that Erich had suggested they pulled a few barnacles off the side of the vessel. In fact it would be a good sport for the locals when these great beasts steamed through the Grand Canal.

As evening came, Erich and Stuart began to worry about their next report to me. They had not observed the two in question all day and assumed they were still in their suite. Reception told them that their quarry had checked out, and yet they had been on the ball, so to speak, all day and had definitely not been passed by. Due to Ciao Bella's size it was unlikely they would have missed them moving in disguise out of the hotel, never mind with luggage.

They could just not believe it; how the hell had the buggers got out? The room key was acquired with a little persuasion *and a gift or two handed over. The suite was inspected and the evidence suggested they had definitely left the building with no intention of returning in the near future. Frustrated, they left the hotel and retired to their own digs to discuss and then explain to me how they had lost the persons of interest.*

It came to Erich that night, while trying to sleep. He was trying to imagine how the hell Robinson and Bella had done their bunk; then it dawned on him: they would have just walked off the balcony onto one of the cargo vessels that had gone right past the hotel as it navigated up the Grand Canal. Now they were going to have to go to the Italian authorities and find out what vessels had been scheduled through that day. They would need the destinations of each to start to try and fathom it all out.

That telegram and telephone call did not make me particularly happy. We had enough at our end to deal with.

It took the boys another two days to narrow it down to two vessels. They flipped a coin and went their separate ways to the ships' relative destinations. Erich headed off to Cyprus, knowing it was going to be a bugger to catch the best transports but he would find his way there - with luck, before the vessel moved on to its next trip. Stuart had lost the coin toss and was now off to India and so would soon be sitting in an aeroplane, relaxing. He would be arriving well before the vessel, giving him plenty of time to snoop.

Chapter 19: Boarding

In the meantime, Berty, with a little help from the military, had acquired photographs of most of Robinson's vessels at sea. The ones without the new hatch above the engine rooms were discounted as potential targets for us to board. We knew there were three of these units to find and render less efficient than the designer's intention. We could not affect the potential effectiveness of the projectile but if we could stop it being launched that would be just the ticket.

Whilst the idea of a plan had been germinated and discussed before Erich and Stuart had left to follow Robinson, no target had been located. Now we had our first target: she was steaming across the Atlantic from Philadelphia on the Eastern seaboard of the USA. Her actual cargo was steel and printing paper; she had done a little cargo exchange in Bordeaux and now was steaming up the west coast of France and Portugal. We knew from the submitted papers that she was on her way to Italy, to the Port of Messina and then on to Venetian being the port of Venice. I did not care what she was carrying; we just needed to be ready to catch a weather window to execute the plan.

Little Alex had arrived while I had sent Berty off to follow the Robinson vessel. He had a high-powered wireless that could get through to our receivers from the motor launch we had hired. He had two of Wing Commander Jack's people with him as they kept just out of sight from the vessel's lookouts. We had learned in Brest that these vessels had no radar so a quick night boarding stood a good chance if it was not expected and the sea was calm.

Berty had all the kit with him that he had designed and built with Charles. There were last minute things to do with the hired launch but these things were being dealt with.

Holding tackle and anchor points were loaded and fitted to the stern of this little motor launch. They bobbed and bounced around in the Atlantic; Berty and the two crew members with him would have preferred it at least a bit calmer. They had a good idea of the prey's destination but needed to follow as close as they dared - by night, within half a mile, running lights off, observing the crew at their tasks on the great Liberty ship. She ploughed through the *waves at a steady fourteen knots no matter what the weather, unbelievably strong as it can be in the Bay of Biscay. Once, the waves were capping out at twenty-two feet and the captain just turned her into it and kept going. For Berty and his crew it was hell: fly the upside of the wave and dive over the crest into the trough; hope the bow of the launch did not cut in too deep. This little thirty-six foot plywood, diesel-engined contraption had not been designed or tested for waters of this ferocity. Navigation with this kind of movement had to be kept to dead reckoning; there were no stars to go by as the rain and squalls were too great. It was too rough for them to eat and cook, so they were having a bad time as far as we knew. The forecasts were not too good but we needed that window.*

Alex arrived and it was great to see the little bugger, immaculately dressed as ever in his civvies. He had been found by Wing Commander Charles' boys, working for Special Forces underground in Ireland. He saw me and his little face lit up. His smile was as broad as it could be; he had never hugged me but as I caught sight of him, he was already trotting across our planning room towards me. His head was in my chest, arms around my waist and before I knew what he was doing I was up in the air. The cheeky bugger then shook his head. I realised what he was doing, the perverted little bastard. He blurted out into my bosom a great sigh and groan. As he did this, I drove my thumbs into the cheeky instructor's arteries at the base of his neck, just to remind him I liked to be in control. He let his grip around my waist go, dropping me to the ground. As my arms transmitted all my eight stones of weight through my thumbs into the base of his neck, he relaxed his knees just a little, while raising his arms in a centred, upward movement then rolling them out in the shape of a wheel. This action forced my arms out, over and away from his shoulders before he blacked out. As my arms relaxed and rolled away, I dropped to the floor and on to one knee, thrusting my right arm forward in a karate style full thrust lockout punch. It was sent out at around fifteen degrees above horizontal and aimed directly at his scrotum. In the milliseconds it took my arm to lock out, he had contracted his calf muscles, flicked his little feet and straightened his knees out. His legs opened wide and his crotch became just out of reach as he tightened his abdominal muscles and drew his hips and so groin away from my reach.

We tag boxed for a few seconds and he said loudly as we did so, "It is you; thank God you are alive. I had hoped that it would be, and I would get to work with you. Get me out of the job I'm in and I'll follow you to hell and back, then I'll turn and put the devil's fire out!"

"That's good enough for me, Sir."

"It's Alex now to you. I see you have lost none of your direct aggression; that makes me happy! So tell me: how do I get involved with your outfit?" He gently straightened his double-breasted suit jacket; straightened his tie; pulled the cuffs of his shirt down to his wrist under the jacket *sleeves; smiled and took his hat off, placing it on the desk in front of him. Those around us just looked at us, stunned by the few seconds of intense combat that had been played through in front of their eyes.*

I laughed; part of my still being alive was due to him and now I was going to ask him to risk his life - but not before I knew what he had been up to.

Although it was not my place to debrief little Alex, I needed to know what he had been up to after World War II had finished. We were both still contracted to the Official Secrets Act and so should not be talking to each other regarding missions and action, but I needed to know if he was still the tiny, steely man I needed.

It came to light he had been working incognito (even with those eyes!), hunting down persons who were connected to the Irish Republican Army and other organisations who had been receiving arms from the UK mainland and moving them across the border, then shipping the stuff to Germany via places such as Lisbon, in Portugal. Quite a few had been caught but there were a few who had moved on before the war was over. It was thought that those were not in Ireland; after his investigations in the really seedy parts of Ulster, the shipyards, the pubs and the rest of Northern Ireland, he had left the country. He must have been going through it and had been living over there under cover for six years. What a way to live. It was not for me!

Alex had come to the conclusion that there some they would never dig out and there were some who would come to light once they sourced where funding was coming from. These persons had scattered all over the globe, he thought: Australia, New Zealand, Canada, the United States and who knew where else? They had probably gone underground, taken jobs and started to raise funds as well as recruit people. Who knew when they would surface and cause havoc? I understood from his expressionless face that he had had the heart ripped out of him. He was still the same man and still had the skill, but he really did need to be part of a team again and not just a spearhead, probing dangerous and violent entities.

His only comment was: "Those who are involved lie; and you can tell when they're lying!"

So I asked, "Come on, tell me!" and

he looked at me with the most serious, dour face and said, "Because, young lady, their lips will be moving!"

It broke the ice and we were on track. I told him about myself and he said he thought there had always been an ulterior motive for my joining and training with the SOE and that was fine with him.

So I started to go through plan one with him and two days later we were on our way to Bordeaux, hoping for that weather window and to catch up with Berty and his crew on the launch. They were going to rendezvous with a ship presently in Bordeaux and take on several drums of fuel as well as the two of us. Then it would be down to the weather to give us the green light. Wing Commander Jack knew the plan; he was not too happy, but in for a penny...

Over the next two days, the weather became calmer and those big Atlantic winds died right down. Blue skies appeared and it was time to look at the job from a better angle. Berty had to be on shift, as he was the only one I knew I could trust at the wheel when we were trying out this new contraption. As we broke out the kite thing that Berty and Charles had built, the others just looked at us and shook their heads. Alex was full of beans but didn't look at the contraption. Thousands of yards of a new nylon rope were laid onto spools. Bert assured me he had tested the stuff for strength and all was well.

We ran a test flight of the unit off the back of the launch into the slight breeze and were able to drop back from the target

Liberty ship to eight miles. This allowed me to look over her from a height through my Zeiss binoculars without being seen by their lookouts. In general, her lookouts would be looking in the direction of travel and various vectors off that up to two hundred degrees around. It was unlikely they would be looking aft!

The kite flew well and controlled well at the height I was working at. We knew it would take the combined weight of Alex and me as Berty was about that. We would have a knife each and a pair of pliers each; other than that, just our hands. We had never worked together in this sense so we went through signalling and how to cover each other, then through the original blueprints of a Liberty ship so that Alex knew the layout as best as was possible. We would go that night, under the cover of darkness. There no point in blacking up, as once we were on board the vessel and inside, the lighting would be quite substantial. The standard shift pattern on most seagoing vessels is that the night watch starts at around 2200 hrs. I wanted to gain access to the ship around 0100 hrs, as this would be their tired point; they would be least likely to be totally alert.

Alex and I dressed in warm but light clothing and light footwear with the most flexibility. Our only precaution was two deflated rubber flotation devices. In actual fact they were the inner tubes from wheelbarrows with the Schrader valves removed. We would have to blow them up by mouth and then get the valve caps screwed on as quickly as we could. Two each, just in *case one was punctured. The aim was to be on and off the vessel in fifteen minutes.*

Berty would follow the vessel as close as he dared, and the two crew members would strain their eyes to see us jump. They would then pick us up as they motored by. Alex and I carried one waxed up (to waterproof it) torch each.

This was it: we were off.

Alex was in a Bosun's chair behind me in the harness that Charles had made. The line was attached to the kite with a quick release and my throat mic was tested for communication with Berty. The launch was turned a little into the wind until we were airborne. At one hundred feet, all was running well and in control; more line was played out. Eventually we were roughly two thousand feet behind the launch and Berty slowly swung the boat to starboard. The idea was that we would then be on his port side and, as a water skier does, we would cut through the air using the sail above us. The launch would be positioned just a little ahead of the target vessel and we would release from directly behind it. Then we would fly directly above her stern and drop onto the deck silently to get on with our work.

All ran beautifully! I called in to the launch, "Finals," dropped the towline and we were on our way. We only had a hundred yards or so to glide down to the ship. I had to adjust to starboard with a few gentle partial turns just to stay lined up correctly for our approach. Berty would retrieve the line but the kite would be lost as it fell into the wake of the ship and be twisted and mangled in the man-made torrent of water behind the vessel. It would find its way to the bottom of this cold, dark, watery grave.

The ship's running lights gave me the most vivid target and so far it was all a piece of cake; easy as she goes. Just above the ships railings on the stern, I tagged Alex to be ready to lose the kite and we would drop to the deck silently. Five feet in over the stern rails, I let it go and we dropped.

Just as we did so, a mass of lights illuminated the stern as if it were daylight. We were blown! It was too late to drop back or catch our sail again; our commitment was too great. As we were free-falling for the last few feet and our eyes adjusted to the lights, we saw the wires, woven like a net. My heart was lost; we were sitting ducks and the most I could think in such a short time was that we were captured. Only God could know what that was going to mean for us! Glancing up, I saw a man with his hands outstretched to two levers, one for the lights and the other - who knew? He had been waiting for us. But how could he have known we were coming? I looked desperately for a way out.

As we hit the wires, we started to scramble across them.

I heard someone shout, "Now!" and the other switch or lever was thrown. We were earthing the wires to each other; the electric shock caused muscular contractions for both of us. The agonising pain was unbelievable; electric blue light flashed around us like lightning.

The lights on this deck were doused

and our observers enjoyed the electric blue light show of our bodies contracting in spasms. There was nothing we could do but die; there was no way we could stop completing the circuit between the wires as we rolled back, towards the top of the railing, then over the stern of the ship.

Down, down we fell towards the churning, fluorescent wake of the ship. Once in the water, with no time to take a breath, the churning fluid drove us both down, deeper and deeper into the dark, ice-cold water. Neither of us had the chance or enough wits about us to attempt to get our flotation devices. We were rolling, turning, tumbling and just hoping there was enough air in our lungs to eventually rise to the surface. I even started to pray, in those few seconds that seemed like a lifetime.

Eventually I found myself gasping for air, but at least I was on the surface of the vast ocean. Treading water, I slowly regained my composure and got enough air into each inner tube to maintain a little extra buoyancy. Then I got my torch out and started to look for Alex. He was a traumatised man, but we were both alive and that was a start. We now needed to stay together and stay calm; recover from the shock, the electrical shock and steady ourselves for the long, hopeful wait. If we were lucky, at least one of the guys on the launch would have seen the stern of the ship light up for those few seconds then the blue flashing of electricity as we made our boarding attempt. If that was so, then it was just possible that they had a pretty good bearing on us and were on their way to pick us up. They could only come and search; for all they knew, we could be dead, captured or have gone over the side into the deep. But Berty would look for me right through the daylight of the next day before he gave up and left my body consigned to the inky, grey-blue salty mass of water.

At best, the two of us had forty, maybe forty-five minutes to live before hypothermia took us to that quiet, peaceful, non-retrievable sleep of lifelessness. The two of us understood the dangers of the mission before we set out, but this had never occurred to me as a possibility. Nobody had ever tried to kill me in such a cold and calculating way. This had now become personal. If we survived, Miss Bella and Mr. Robinson would have their last breath at my hands!

Alex and I clung together to try and conserve some body heat, my legs around him and then his around me. As we bobbed up and down in the ocean, we both had our torches out, turned on and pointing into the darkness behind the other. We talked about so much and learned so much about each other as we mumbled to each other and kept our spirits up. I laughed to myself as I now knew that the size of a man's feet has nothing to do with the size of a certain appendage, and I now knew why Alex had so much confidence with women. If he could use that thing most women were going to come back for more; it made me chuckle to remember that night at the dance!

We started to drift in and out of delirium and had to slap each other to keep ourselves going. Twice we heard an engine *and twice it went by us. We fought for a long time and kept going as the daylight started to appear. The third time we heard that engine it very nearly ran over us. The nine-foot swell that we had been rising and falling on had kept us hidden - until the launch nearly dropped its bow onto us. They hove to and got lines to us. They dragged us in and pulled us on board. They stripped us, dried us and got us into the small cabin. Rough wool blankets were thrown over us and two of the crew started to rub us both all over to create some heat. It was not just to keep us alive; they needed to get that red, viscous fluid flowing around the body with enthusiasm. If not there was a good chance that gangrene might set in and the loss of limbs was a real possibility. I was too far gone to comprehend this. It was great to be* in good hands; they were on the ball enough to understand the possibilities. They weren't going to let us sleep until they got some hot, sweet fluids into us. Then hot food was forced down our throats. Alex and I were then both allowed to collapse into a deep, long, uninterrupted, warm, living sleep.

When I awoke, I started to debrief Berty. He was shocked and then he confirmed everything that had happened with Alex in his own words. The conclusion - other than it was all a disaster - was that we must have a mole in the team. Berty, Alex, Charles and I could be the only persons now who could know anything and be trusted. Even Jack could be the snake in the grass. Holy doodahs! Where the hell did we start with this box of frogs? Berty dismantled the wireless on the launch and took the little

*vessel back to Bordeaux. Here we
disembarked and all five of us headed to
Dole and sanctuary with Charles.*

*Once Charles was aware of the
situation we agreed that Berty would go
back to the UK and start trying to wheedle
out the traitor. In the meantime, it would be
allowed to be understood that Alex and I
were missing in action and that our fate was
unknown. The two crew members who had
been with Berty would have to stay with us
as it had to be recognised that they might be
the traitors. Trust was going to have to be
earned and would not be granted until all
this had been cleared up.*

Berty headed back to the UK in the reliable
Travant. Firstly he went north to see Jack
and give him the news. As he travelled, he

had time to think and in his mind he narrowed a few things down. Kuzman could have talked to JJ and that was a possibility, knowing she had contact with Robinson. Yet Kuzman did not know how the attack was going to be executed. Brown was a definite possibility if he had been snooping or listening; yet the lanky, insipid, cheating accountant who knew Robinson and Bella could not have known anything. As he went through so many scenarios, Berty began to understand that there were only certain persons who had enough information to know who, what, where and when: Jack, Erich, Charles, Stuart, Alex, Berty himself and Murtyl. Nothing had ever been put down on paper and blackboards had always been wiped down with a damp cloth.

Jack was upset about Murtyl and

would not accept Murtyl had gone. He would not arrange a funeral with honours and would not inform Murtyl's grandma. The mission would play out and then this disaster would be dealt with. The endgame was all that mattered. Murtyl had known the risks and it had been agreed at the beginning that these things were a real possibility. Berty understood his stance and desperately wanted to let Jack in on the knowledge but it had not been agreed with Murtyl. Jack was openly devastated and took a ramrod position in driving everything forward. He stepped up and took control of the whole operation with Berty.

The thumbscrews were tightened and everybody was made to work longer days, dig deeper and push to bring this whole thing to an end.

Chapter 20: Images

While in the north, Berty wanted to know more about the work Blyth had been doing for Robinson. The work needed to carry on but he wanted to understand what else was happening in those workshops. If there was going to be another pickup from Tees docks, when would it be? This was probably the last chance they were going to have unless Stuart or Erich came up with something. Blyth met with Bert and brought Kuzman with him. Berty wanted to know why Kuzman was there and Blyth pointed out that Kuzman ran the workshops and had every reason to despise the way his work was being used. All of the Accelerator guns had gone but there were parts of the miniaturised nuclear plant left. This had to be shipped somewhere, installed and put on line. So there was one last chance to follow them to whatever base Robinson had. It kept running through his mind: how had they known about the attack? All the time, he worried about how things were to progress.

In the meantime, the poor Ghanaian slaves had kept digging out the iron and silicate-rich rock in the Hellenic arc. It was always warm and they were worked to exhaustion. Most of the workable rich ore had gone, being shipped by Robinson's ships. The ships had arrived heavy in the water but now often came in carrying a lot of ballast. The machinery was in; the defences had been installed, as had the Accelerator gun. All that was left was to bring in the nuclear fission plant; install it;

commission and connect it to the generator. It would supply Robinson's home turf with pretty much limitless electrical power to do as he chose for many, many years to come. The labyrinth of chambers in this hewn out rock contained workshops, machinery, smelters, living quarters and an infirmary - in fact it was now a small city, hidden away from prying eyes.

Robinson and Bella had made a show of not knowing they had been onto them and had then snapped the jaws of hell on Murtyl's team's first attempt. The only ace up the sleeve was that Murtyl was alive and they did not know. It had to stay that way!

While Kuzman and Blyth tried to produce a date for Berty to work on regarding the last shipment for Robinson, he flicked through a few old images he kept in his wallet, remembering the things Murtyl, the team and he had gone through in 1945. He placed them on the desk in front of him and rose lethargically from his chair to go and make a mug of tea for each of them. The photographs were left on the desk and Kuzman glanced up and asked if he could look at them. He wanted to see how bedraggled Murtyl and her team had become at the end of the war; what it had done to them and how they looked on the day of the great race in Paris on September 15th, 1945.

Berty waved a hand as if to say: of course you can. Kuzman leant forward and drew the pictures towards him. He thumbed through them slowly and smiled at the sight of team members who obviously worked so closely together. He squinted a little and then walked off, returning with a magnifying glass. Scratching his head, he pondered for a few seconds and then started to count on his fingers. He wanted to know if Berty knew when Murtyl had teamed up with these two guys in Switzerland. Berty said he did not know but it had to be after her landing date in France late in 1944.

Kuzman became more and more perturbed and fidgety and eventually Peter boomed out with, "Sit still, man! What the hell is up with you?"

Kuzman replied with a most unexpected response: "I know this man; he came here to these workshops in 1943."

Berty nearly dropped the tea and jumped toward the grand desk. "Who?" he asked, almost shouting at Kuzman.

Kuzman pointed. "He is the Irishman that came with Robinson to understand the units that went to Ireland and who, we know now, then went to Saint Omer in France for the Nazis."

"That cannot be! That man, Stuart, fought with us in France against the Nazis!" said Berty.

"But this is him, I know him. I met him and the dates fit. I have been working them out and I know I am correct. You could verify it by asking JJ to look at the picture. She went out for a drink with him during the few days he was here. I remember, as it upset me at the time."

The next day the photographs were placed in front of JJ and she confirmed Brian's statement. Berty left, dragging Brian with him. Peter was left in his office, not in shock, but with no number one to run the show as it were. Brian Kuzman was taken to his home to grab a few things.

Twenty-four hours later, he was sitting in front of a live Murtyl in the monastery at Dole.

He told his story to me and I slammed my fist down on the table. How the hell could this be Stuart? I could not figure it out. Alex stood behind me and was looking from the side as he could not see over my shoulder. He came out with a few choice words and then started to reel off some history:

"This man was not Stuart Lattimer at all. It was actually Seamus Stuart Lattimer, born in Belfast and known to be a very militant man. He went missing from Northern Ireland early in 1944, after several

bodies were found in the Harland & Wolff shipyard. It was not the murders he was primarily wanted for, but the possibility of being a Nazi sympathiser. This type were often sent abroad to start again; be out of the way; start businesses to raise monies to fund the activists or recruit for them. That was probably why he was in Switzerland, but he was known to be addicted to violence.

"He liked to fight hand to hand, with weapons, but loved to blow things up. That would fit his style and I can see why he would work well with you in the field as you had no idea about his true history or agenda. There would be a slightly different personal moral code going on. I want to talk with him now, initially about our recent dip in the drink and experiences, but also about his past. He will be heading to the courts and imprisonment or he can have what is just; so many have died or had their lives destroyed by so called sympathisers!

We all looked at each other. I felt abused, and my trust so badly misused, but it ticked all the boxes and made sense.

Berty nodded a solemn nod and said, "Brian, I'm sorry. You can find your own way home. Tell nobody that Murtyl is alive! Murtyl and I will go to Paris tomorrow. Alex, Murtyl and myself to India now! I want a word with Stuart, or Seamus, or whatever his name is!"

I said, "Actually Brian, we can all go to Paris together. Why don't you invite JJ over and have few days in Paris with her, then head back home? I will clear it with Peter and Wing Commander Jack can foot the bill. JJ would seem to be straight enough *and you can get that relationship running smoothly, if you know what I mean. Mr. and Mrs. Norman Brown, I will deal with when this is all over. Just keep in mind who they are and tell no one. Is that all OK with you, Brian?"*

Brian replied, "Yes. I'm sure JJ would like the break and I know I will relax a bit, but are you sure we cannot help?"

"No, I can't have you get in the way when we start the last phase of the operation," I said.

That afternoon we travelled towards Paris in the Travant, making the best pace we could.

Chapter 21: India – and to the Island

After six weeks of research every weekend, poor little Phillipa was beginning to wonder how many lives Murtyl had. She had had one evening off to go and start the little race car they had rebuilt. They had not been to its first race and had not seen it being run in. Seemingly it had gone well but that was not the same as being there.

"Dad, why is Murtyl the one who takes all the risks?" asked Phillipa of her father.

"Well Sweetheart, there are those who do in life and there are those who sit on their great shiny backsides and would like to think they do! Murtyl was decisive and had her own, very strong moral code. If she could not, she would not ask anyone else to do something."

"Dad, I understand all that, I'm not nine years old any more. It's just that I'm struggling to cope with what she goes through. If I fell off the back of a ship, I don't think I would survive!"

"No, I'm in the same boat. Ha! Same boat! Get it?"

"Yes Dad, very good – not!"

"Cheeky! But yes, I understand; all the same, they were a different breed of people back then. In her case just a complete blinking one-off. If she jumped out of an aeroplane with no 'chute, somehow she would be OK."

"But Dad, she never makes a mistake and when we do this research it's always verified and validated. I'm getting really worried that she won't survive!"

"Well, stupid, she will; because you're getting so involved, you are forgetting that this is her second diary, and to write a diary you must have got to the end. Also I know there are several more. But more importantly, I knew her and she was real!"

"Yes Dad, but we both worry about her. You have not been to the Wheat, The Kind or The Bay in weeks. Can we have a rest for a few days? You have school and I have work and then we do this all weekend. I think we both need a break."

Her dad replied, "Pip, if you're that mixed up that you have me going to school and you working, then you're right; let's have a day out! Then you and I can get cracked on and have some fun together. Is there anything you would like to do?"

"You let me think about that for ten seconds, while I have a look at this calendar. Yes – here we go. Tomorrow, the lads are out at Oulton Park. It takes two and a quarter hours to get there and we can leave here at seven. I can get you up if you sleep in and we can see how they perform. It's a quick but tight track and I can look after the stopwatches. Is that OK with you?"

"It would seem, young lady, that the decision has been made. If I fill the car up today, we can get a straight start in the morning."

"Then that's settled. What are the chances of me getting a lap or two with someone at the lunch break? It would be better for me to know the track more, for when I start racing, don't you think Dad?"

"Yes it probably would, but who is going to pay for our racing when you hit the heady heights of sixteen?"

"Come on Dad, you are. You're on the engine; the lads are on the body, brakes and set up. I'm behind the wheel and then on the podium! Easy!"

"In your eye I suppose it is. I can't say we'll see, but we can try for base scenario. You will have to do well in your exams, though!"

"Dad they're six years off, and you know my thoughts on tests and exams: there are no easy or hard answers to questions. You either know the answer or you don't. In this case I do, we will and I am! Good enough?"

"OK little madam, OK. Now when we get back, are we going to get down to it and get this finished for Murtyl?"

"Oh yes Dad. It's not that I'm jaded, and I'm definitely not bored – just tired. This referencing never stops and I get terrified by some of the things that have actually happened to her!"

"I know Pip, it terrifies me, and I knew her and loved the crazy old bugger!"

*

Bombay. Hot, sweaty, sticky and a little fruity on the smelly side compared to what we were used to. The streets were busy and we needed to keep a low profile until the vessel in question had left the port. We watched from a distance and sure enough, as she was unloaded, many things that had been exported from Europe were not being unloaded. The weights were the same but the actual units were completely different.

It was a very discreet smuggling operation, shipping tons of gold and other precious metals and getting maybe twice what it was worth in the more developed parts of the world. The rest of the cargo went through the normal process of disembarking but we kept watch.

Then the clincher happened. Alex caught it on his watch. We had a hotel with an overview of the docks where our vessel of interest was unloading. Going out was not an option, as we could not afford to be spotted. I was dead, remember - although if we had had some kit with us it would have been a good port to have a crack at her.

Anyway, Alex called us both out from our resting positions in different parts of the suite. Neither of us was particularly alert but we rose and came to have a look through the one set of binoculars we had between us. First Berty took a sighting then I had a look. Seamus - to Alex - and Stuart to us was scampering up the gangplank, chatting to the first mate. For me it was not necessarily conclusive, as he could have been doing what I would have liked him to - although it was more than suspicious! I needed to stay out of sight with Berty. Then once the ship had sailed we could allow Alex to accidentally bump into Stuart. We would see what the outcome was and then walk in after listening to them chatting. Ideally, if we could watch, that would even better.

Another day or two went past while we remained hot and bothered. We consumed curry after curry and drank Coke after Coke as we needed to be sure none of us was going to end up with that dicky tummy you so often hear about from not such good water.

The ship sailed on the evening tide. Stuart had actually spent a day or two on the vessel, leaving it as she loosed her mooring from the dock.

It was dark; in fact pitch black (if they had pitch there I did not know!) There was no street lighting and the doorways and shop fronts were all full of living skeletons who chased you for money, food - anything. It was a tough area to be in.

Alex followed Seamus as he walked through the dark streets around the port. We assumed he was on his way back to his hotel, but no: he was going down to see all the thieves and vagabonds. The area was dark and just occasionally, if you turned your head, you would see the tell-tale pairs of red dots - the eyes of brown rats watching you as you passed, not even disturbed from their foraging activities. It gave me the shivers!

As Stuart rounded one particular corner and Alex was following close enough to have a go, he did. It was right at the open area that I think must have been a sort of abattoir.

Alex had sidled up behind Stuart and called out with an impeccable Irish accent, "Seamus, Seamus is that you?" Sure enough Stuart turned around on his heels with a broad smile and looked at Alex. His eyes rolled as Stuart realised he did not know Alex. Alex stepped forward and Stuart went to draw something from his pocket. Alex leapt forward and had Stuart's arms smothered before he even got to draw whatever he was aiming to bring out. The rabbit punches started just as I had seen them being thrown by Alex before. This time they travelled a quarter-inch further. Stuart seemed to vibrate or shudder in the dim light. Then he rolled, his knees went and the sack of spuds look-alike routine started again.

Once down on the deck, Berty and I strolled into a closer proximity to watch and listen more closely. Alex pulled a cut-throat razor out of his rear pocket and started to cut the clothes off Stuart. Once Stuart was naked, Alex took his own shoes and socks off.

He looked up at the two of us and said very quietly, "Don't be shocked; don't *butt in; just listen. This is the only way to deal with these indoctrinated psychopaths."*

I stood there, stunned to think he could say that about Stuart. Calmly, Alex took the right arm of what appeared to be a corpse and placed it at a right angle up behind the back. Then he rolled the body onto its back. Standing on the side with the arm tucked under the back, he placed his left foot's big toe in the body's neck. The ball of his foot was placing pressure on the carotid artery. He raised the right leg of the body and pulled it up towards himself. Then he cut the right leg's Achilles tendon.

I was shocked at the barbarity of Alex, who looked at me and said, "You have no idea who this really is, do you? He was one of the ringleaders and is probably responsible for many tons of British ordnance landing on and killing the Allies through World War II. He will tell you this when he comes round. He can't run; he has eight broken ribs and is going to struggle to breathe. He will be praying I allow him to go to hospital, but that will be his choice. You need to know who, what, where, when and why he - just a few days ago - nearly had you and me killed! Got it?"

"Yes Alex, I think I have."

The body started to come round, moaning and stirring as he began to feel the pain from the blows he had been assaulted with. His eyelids lifted and then stared up at Alex with absolute contempt. We stayed out of sight! The cut-throat razor in Alex's skilled hand started to shave the hairs from the inside of Stuart's leg. Stuart went to struggle and break free; his arm screamed at him not to move, his ribs moved and delivered the same message to his brain and he stopped.

Alex began to ask questions. Confirmation of his real name came with ferocity of unmentionable verbal abuse and high-speed sputum. Alex looked at him calmly and told him he had a surprise for him - once he got the information he required; that he knew ninety percent of the answers and just wanted to fill in a few blanks. He knew that Stuart had been in Ireland and had visited Middlesbrough several times during World War II. The Accelerator guns had gone to Ireland to be shipped on. Three were now with SR Enterprises on vessels and they knew about the nuclear materials. He wanted to know who his contacts were in Ireland, where he sent the funds he produced when in Switzerland and where Robinson's actual place of residence was.

It took a while before he started to give in and give Alex the information required. Stuart - or Seamus - was actually holding up quite well until I saw one thing I had never seen or heard of before. He had passed out a few times when Alex had placed just enough pressure on the artery to starve the brain of blood so he started to lose consciousness. Then his body relaxed and fluids and so on were released. Every time his body lost that conscious state, Alex dipped the end of his razor in the brown stuff and smeared a little up Seamus's nose. The ammonia acted like smelling salts and brought him straight back round. There was going to be no rest until Alex had what he wanted; it went on for fifty or so minutes.

We stepped forward into the dim light where Seamus could see us. His eyes became wide with hatred and it was over for me.

Seamus shouted at me, wanting to know, "Why won't you just lie down and die?"

Berty and I left and Alex followed; either the rats or infection would do for him or he might survive. I didn't care; we knew the names of the vessels, where our leak had come from and the island the miniature nuclear power plant had gone to and so probably the location of the third weapon. It was time to regroup and assess the situation again. They wouldn't be looking for Seamus to make contact now for several weeks unless we were making a move. At last we had the advantage and it was time to press that home, clean and hard.

Just a note: I hate and loathe no races, creeds or nationalities. They all have my trust and I have worked with most. But to be misled, lied to or used is, and never will be, acceptable in my book.

Back to the UK to bring Jack, Peter and Brian up to speed with the whole affair. Now that we possibly had the location, we needed to understand the reason for being at that location. It might just explain a lot to us very quickly. Once back in our coincidence room, we looked at a few map references and charts.

A few things at last became clear.

The island was very small, situated off the

end of Cyprus. The first thing to do was draw a circle around it at one hundred and seventy-five miles. That might give us a clue as to what the Accelerator gun could be aimed at. Used as a defence it was too big, too slow and too inaccurate. As a stealth attack weapon, it would be unbelievably devastating and impossible to defend against. The ring covered a lot of water and a few areas of landmass that was known to be oil-rich. It also just scraped over Tel Aviv. Tel Aviv had to be the first target. Nuclear weapon, X kilotons - just what that Nazi lot would have been looking to do: start the ruddy war all over again with some other damned 'Reich'.

We needed to reccy the island and work out an attack plan. We also needed to work at finding the vessels fitted with the guns, but at least we knew their names now, courtesy of Seamus. The two ships would have to be dealt with differently to our previous attempt. They would be alert to us, but not to the day or the time of our attacks as their inside man would not be communicating with them.

The island would take a few days or more to survey. There were ways of entry to be looked at; how to land without suspicion; where their sea defences were; how many personnel would be required; what demolition devices and sizes would be needed. No matter how much we got from maps and observation, there was going to be a lot of guesswork involved. It was not the best way to start an operation but it was what we had.

Wing Commander Jack helped with a

solution to help us without being reduced too much in manpower by talking to Beetle, who now needed to be in the loop, as it were. Beetle and Jack had had a telephone discussion over their scramblers. Beetle soon became aware of the situation but was shocked at the size and potential danger to the world. He proffered all the support required and more. He would not go to all the other persons from the original meeting in France, just in case there was a leak there. The first move was to get one of the US submarines that they just happened to have in the Mediterranean to keep a watch on all movement around and on the island.

The island was pretty much separated into two halves: one private and industrial and the other a pretty popular resort and fishing village. Ideally it would be best if Robinson was on the island when we moved to his facilities and took possession, but we were unable to confirm that over the several days of observation.

We had persons observing while posing as tourists out walking, to see what kind of land defences had been put in. We watched from the water: several fishing vessels were hired to sail continuously past the seaward entrance. We could see they had radar built in so no metal or powered vessels could be used to get in. While this was going on, with extreme effort not to be detected, Berty, Alex, a very shocked Erich (at the loss of his friend) and I went after the two vessels.

Chapter 22: Into Action

We could not hope to get at either vessel while at sea and on the move - it was going to have to be at anchor or in port. Either would be fine as long we had time to do what we needed without being detected. We were going to have to be in and out like ghosts. It was going to be tough but we had the new Lungs from Cousteau, the compressors and the pressure relief valves, or regulators as he called them. No rebreathers, which meant as far as I was concerned we had a chance.

We went into both vessels just a few days apart. One had been anchored off Marseilles, which was good for us. Berty knew his way around the area and the port so we were able to get the right kind of access. We were taxied out to the vessel by pilot cutter with the help of the port authorities. On the second vessel the same assistance was given to us by the local customs.

In each case, while the official boarders were climbing up the lowered gangplank and in the other case up the lowered rope ladder, we had gone quietly over the side of the launch. We swam under the vessel and forward to the chains from the bow that led to the anchors. Erich stayed with the air tanks and regulators while Alex, Berty and I went up the heavy, greased link chains and through the lowering eyes on the bow of the ships. Berty then stayed there and guarded our point of exit. Both jobs were done at night and in the case where the pilot cutter had delivered us, we had thirty minutes to get in and out undetected before he started to guide the ship into port under her own propulsion.

Alex and I stripped and dried as fast as we could. Berty removed light, dry clothing and plimsolls from a waxed water-proof bag. We dressed and checked each other out. Berty reminded us of our time restraints and exactly where we were headed, remembering our visit in Brest and the dry-docked vessel in the old submarine pens. Then we were off.

From the bow, we worked our way towards midships along the deck, doing our best not to be seen. The bridge was busy and we could see the officers on that bridge dealing with their visitor. We carried on past the deck cranes and on towards the superstructure, entering it through one of the water sealable door hatches and then working our way through the ship. We were ever watchful not to be located as uninvited guests. Slowly, after a few near misses, we made our way to the engine room.

The engineers were working steadily away, ready to produce power on the demand of the captain and pilot and so their eyes were focused on the job. They remained unaware of us, the intruders to their place of work. None of the crew members we saw were armed and that made me feel a little more secure. It wasn't long before we arrived at the entrance hatch of the specially added room enclosing the Accelerator gun and all its controls. Now was the really risky one; we had no idea of how close they were to firing these things. The room could be alive with personnel and then again it could *also be empty. Alex and I both took a deep breath, I drew a knife and he held out his bare hands, counting one, two...*

...three and we went in, ready for the fight of our lives. I went down and rolled in on the floor, while he came in fast on his feet, eyes searching for the foe.

It was empty! No personnel, no white light - the room was bathed in red light. Alex closed the hatch behind us and the locks gently rotated into place. Then we got to work.

The plans that Kuzman had forced us to memorise were so correct that once we found the firing systems it was uncanny. For me, I thought we were lucky. They had gone for the firing system that was guaranteed, tried and tested on engines the world over. I understood these ignition systems and we quickly had the firing order changed as Brian had required. The drilling that Brian had given us meant it was only access that was difficult. Actually doing the job was second nature for us.

If it had all been on the coloured wires, being the other potential system even Alex would have been sunk. With no time to do tests or tracing and nothing to test with, the coloured wires would have been impossible to read correctly in fixed red light. For us to throw a switch may have alerted our possible captors. Oh, never to be without a torch is something I will never forget. Maybe we should have had torches with us, but it was something else to carry, and something else to drop. Enough noise to be heard but also evidence of our visit. It *had only been a few days before that two little torches had saved our lives. In this situation they also could have been our downfall.*

The vessel started to vibrate and we could feel the big diesel engine being brought to life. We needed to get out of this room and make our way back to Berty, before they started to weigh anchor. Over the bow and into the drink; get our apparatus from Erich and get underway ourselves. We would need to stay underwater for the first few hundred yards to make sure we were not spotted. This all had to be done before she weighed anchor and started to spin that prop. The last thing Alex and I wanted was to be dragged down along the barnacle encrusted hull, having our skin torn off as the ship moved forward, then to be dragged unceremoniously deeper, towards her screw. Then, if not cut to ribbons by that ton-and-a-half bronze propeller and battered to death, we would still have drowned in the turbulence. No set of Aqua-lungs was going to save us here. To have Berty and Erich go through it too would have broken my heart, but then I'd be dead too anyway!

We pushed underwater towards the port as hard as we could for the first few hundred yards and then surfaced. We congratulated each other, firstly because we had completed the mission and there was only one other ship to do, and secondly because the opposition had no idea I was alive. We now had the upper hand; we were going to win!

Chapter 23: Showdown

"Dad, do you think Murtyl was crazy, a bit simple or just addicted to adrenaline?"

Nick answered his wonderful little daughter Pip. "Well Sweetheart, I know you never experienced meeting Murtyl and sadly neither did you know your mum. Your mum was special in ways I can never explain; my connection to her was there from the minute I saw her. I knew what she was thinking before it was said or suggested. I know I look back probably with rose-tinted glasses, but I still feel that connection, for all that she has gone!"

"Did you love Mum, Dad?" asked Pip with that excited enthusiasm only young persons can effervesce with. She was almost bouncing off the chair next to Nick, in front of the computer and their reference work and Murtyl's diary.

"Pip, you know I did, and still do. I miss her every day; I think of her every day and I still see her in my dreams." A tear rolled from Nick's right eye, down to bathe his cheek in warm salty water. Pip ran and pulled out a handkerchief and mopped the wetness away from his stubbly cheek.

"Sorry, Dad. I shouldn't go there I know; it just crept up on me and then fell out before I could stop it!" Pip butted in as she almost shrank away from the pain she could see in her father's eyes.

"It's OK my little angel, come here and give me a hug. Sometimes it's good to be reminded how wonderful life can be. To be with that one person with whom you just synchronise!" replied Nick.

"Dad you're confusing me now. Synchronise - what does that mean?"

"You know how Murtyl would synchronise watches with persons so when they were doing whatever they did, they did it at exactly the same time? She also had that connection to Berty that she refers to so much!"

"Ye-es, I'm following," she replied in a questioning sort of way.

"Well that's what your mum and I had. Our two frequencies matched so perfectly in my eyes. We never argued, and I have to admit that waking up in the morning was the most wonderful experience."

Pip butted in, not sure if she really wanted to know but sort of did: "So why was it then? She can't have brought you Yorkshire tea and toast every morning in bed!" Her little arms were raised and her hands were resting on her hips and. She cocked her head to one side.

"No Pip. But when I opened my eyes, I got to see her face. It raised my game and I always regretted shutting them the night before. I could just look at her and it made me feel warm, loved and just the luckiest man alive. And and now I have you, you cheeky little rascal! You've done it again and got me off track. Where was I? Oh yes: was Murtyl crazy, simple or an adrenaline junky? Hmmm," he hummed, as he stroked his chin with his right hand, looking at Pip. "I suppose I thought she was a little off her rocker at first, but then I realised she just had her own methodical way and routines. If she had been a cleaner you would have just thought she had a bit of flair. Now Murtyl was way past the idea of having a bit of flair. Hunting, shooting, flying, diving, racing and all the dangers she experienced has got to affect you somehow. She had that connection with Berty that was really fantastically special. I think she was about as mad as a beautiful Labrador, laid on her back having her tummy rubbed; just full of love. Although if you threatened anything she believed in, or loved, I think you were going to regret it. She just had very definite morals, and played in an arena that I hope nobody ever has to cope with again. In conclusion: I think she was the strongest, most gentle, loving mechanic I have ever met!"

Pip jumped in: "Mechanic?"

"Yes Pip. As a driver, rider and mechanic she was unbelievable. As a friend and mentor she could not disappoint. But she could - and did - kill people. I know it was different then, in those times! Mechanic is just a different name for it!"

Pip suggested, "You mean like that film we saw from the seventies a few days ago on the Betamax called *The Mechanic* with Charles Bronson from when was it… 1972?"

"Yes Pip; that is the one. You do pay attention now, don't you? I hope you are doing so at school - it's parents' evening soon and I will be checking with Miss Barlow!"

"That's fine Dad, it's all in hand and I have her buttered up just right. You should try it!"

"Thank you Pip that's enough. Let's get on, and maybe in a few days we can look at that Oulton Park excursion. No promises, mind!"

"Lips are moving Dad; eyes down and on the ball please."

Nick chuckled and the digression ceased. He still missed her every day though, as he thought, "Now where were we…"

It came to him quickly: the recce of the landmass had been done extensively while she had been away. The submarine had not been able to surface as the facility had been noted to have radar. A plan had been hatched by those who had been doing the said reconnaissance and Murtyl and the new team looked over it. Parts were fine but she quickly picked holes in so much of it; it was going to be easier to start from scratch.

Getting men to the main entrance was going to be difficult enough, but taking the seven guards out, all within a second or so, was going to be the key. Once that was done, it would be relatively easy to progress until they were discovered and the alarms went off. Then it was going to be difficult as they had no plan of the inside and did not know what to expect.

She could use the little wooden fishing boats by day and night to fish close to their small harbour entrance. They had been doing so anyway and so were to a degree above suspicion. That would place ten or so men within one hundred yards of where they needed to be. They would have Geiger counters to help find the radioactive material. Plastic and weapons for the assault had also arrived. The SAS guys who could use them were also on the island; they would just need briefing.

Approaching by land was difficult off road; there were plenty of discreet fences that were hard to negotiate due to their construction. No mines had been located but there were a few guard posts that made sure you knew you were not welcome. A fairly large road meandered across the island from the fishing village and the tourist area. It was feasible that a drunken party could walk down that road but it was a little off-beat as an idea. It would have been a good idea but as it had probably not happened before, it would have to be ditched.

Erich, Berty, Charles Alex and I went over and over maps of the area and models of the target's entrance. There had been some aerial images taken but they had revealed nothing. It was getting to that despair moment when any damn thing thrown into the hat had to be considered. Then Alex came up with an idea for a diversion. We all looked at him and said there was no way a diversion was going to work. Everything was too tightly packed and organised. The opposition, it had been noted, were all very well trained, and I mean very well! He argued his case, explained parts of the plan and sold it to us well. So according to him, we needed a 'Pat' – whatever that was. He sent for his and it arrived, apparently. He convinced us that no practice run or dummy run would be of help. Once we were committed it would work, and that was that: we were off.

2300 hrs: all was set. The SAS lads were in the fishing boats pretending to fish and making a little noise as if they had been and were drinking.

The four and I - Berty, Erich and the two from the launch - blacked our faces with burnt cork and got as close as we could to the entrance area without being seen. We waited. What we were waiting for was the diversion; pyrotechnics, flash and stun grenades had all been set aside as too dangerous. It was going to be hard enough but the less we had to fight in the end, the better.

Three other small teams went for the pillboxes after going through the wires and then stayed out of sight until the 'Pat' happened. Alex would join us after the 'Pat' thing; we stayed hidden and waited, not *knowing what to expect.*

Then he appeared, walking down the road and looking a little worse for wear. Holding his arm was an extremely voluptuous woman. My thoughts were: "The stupid idiot's got the wrong night! We're sunk and we'll have to go again tomorrow- if we can get out without being seen."

This woman was exquisitely dressed, I have to say, and was not one of the local ladies of the night! They walked past me, within a few feet of reach. She smelled great and it wasn't Castrol R; it was proper fancy stuff from Paris, probably! Her hair was up, held under a beret, I thought. Her eyes were large and dark brown, her face oval in shape with strong, prominent cheekbones. Her makeup, as far as I could see, was just right: the lips were red, and full - as was her

438

chest. Over a blouse she wore a short waistcoat, emphasising her bosom. Her narrow waist accentuated her smoothly rounded hips, which in turn supported the tightest backside I had ever seen. Her legs were not too long but for her five feet four inches were just about right; they were slender, with black lines running down the back of what I presumed to be fishnet stockings. Those legs ran down into extremely high, black stiletto shoes of the type I wouldn't even try to walk in. She looked good next to Alex as she swung her hips like a right madam.

As he levelled with me, he stopped this lady, looked right at my eyes and whispered, "Meet 'Pat'!"

I snapped back through gritted teeth, "What the hell?"

439

And they walked on without breaking their stride.

I found out just a few moments later that she appeared to be a little tipsy; he pulled a small flask out of his pocket and offered her a drink. She took it and said very politely that she was grateful - then downed it in one. It had begun: within a few seconds, Alex had danced around her and stuck his thumb up towards me with his back to the guards close by. They were all watching now and all I could do was wait to see what was about to unfold.

Pat's hips started to move a little bit more; her arms came up and gracefully she took hold of the beret and removed it, rolling it around her finger a few times and then dispatching it over the wall closest to her. Her hands ran down over her torso, following the shape of her body as she shook her hair free from the beret, allowing it to cascade over her shoulders. The waistcoat was unbuttoned as she danced around Alex. I've never seen such a seductive creature flaunting all her attributes. The show carried on as they wandered even closer to the guarded area. More and more of her clothing was loosened and lost in all directions. I could hardly take my eyes off this mind-numbing set of movements.

Then it hit me: my eyes were supposed to be somewhere else! The guards were supposed to be watching this fabulous show, while we moved in a little closer. So as long as all the guards were heterosexual, we needed to be moving. They were. The show only lasted five minutes or so. Our focus was on getting behind the guards. Their individual attention was nearly all on supporting the wrong weapon, if you know what I mean!

It took a second or so to get the lads' attention then we moved in and worked our way around the absorbed guards. Once we were behind them, each was coshed hard just behind the ear. The guards were physically stunned and I now understood why Alex had wanted a 'Pat' diversion, as he had put it. Those guards had been mesmerised by the show and we were now past the first hurdle. Alex caught up with us at the entrance to the stronghold, took his jacket off and showed me he was ready to go once he had blacked up. He had his tools: a gun, cosh, knuckle duster and knife.

I started to say to him, "What the..?"

and was interrupted with an answer from Alex: "Pat's my wife. With the right stimulant, that's what happens. You can't stop it and she never remembers. It's one of the reasons I married her: good at parties but a stopper if you need it. Whenever I can, I get her away for few days' holiday. This year this is it! We can leave her now; Pat will sit on the wall until I come out and take her back to the hotel."

We went in through the doors and started to take the place to bits. We were followed by the SAS boys and their demolition equipment.

It was a room by room fight now. As we took their guys down, we acquired their high-tech machine guns which evened things up a bit. Once the enemy started to thin out a bit in numbers and we had progressed a little into the complex, the SAS boys started to lay charges in the appropriate corners and uprights of the complex. As we moved forward and got closer to what I thought must be the firing or command centre, things intensified. Hand-to-hand fighting started and, against the odds, my lads began to gain the upper hand.

In the very few fractions of seconds I had occasionally to look up, I saw that Alex was getting inside his opposition range and then doing what he did best -exploding in an uncontainable manner until they fell. Berty, bless him, was doing his own thing, getting closer and closer to the entrance. Twice that I now knew of, he had thrown knives to drop an assailant coming at me from a direction out of vision to me. The other two guys were doing themselves proud fighting with Erich.

The Geiger counter was giving a reading so there had to be nuclear material in the vicinity. The only question was, where? Robinson had to be found, stopped and this deadly material recovered. Or at least, that was the brief!

Berty forced the door open enough for me to squeeze through into the control room. His job was to come in with me but the gap was too small; Alex would have to come through to help when he got here. In the meantime, Berty could help clear out the rest and then, with Erich, destroy the Accelerator gun. It got complicated for them when they started to open the cells with the Ghanaians in. Some were fit enough to want to help and they did so, fighting like demons and picking

445

up anything and attacking whoever they knew to be from this establishment. The guards were dressed in military style uniform but we were now coming across technicians who were dressed in black laboratory coats. Some had a silver cross embroidered on the left breast, with 'SS' embroidered too, just below. Others, who were much more frightened, had the Star of David embroidered in the same place. They were all herded away as much as possible while the real fighting went on. In the brightly lit control room there were four persons. Two were dispatched before I met my match.

Then there she was: the dainty, deadly Miss Bella stood before me. She grinned that broad, lipsticked smile. Under one arm she held a Luger pistol. It had a rifle butt attachment to the pistol grip and a double length magazine. If it was fully loaded, she had up to eighteen shots available and I was her only target.

I had nothing left. I was worn out and my last knife had gone. All that was available to me was the wooden bobbin holding my hair up and in place, out of the way.

But instead of pulling the trigger and flattening me, Miss Bella was listening to the over-confident, smooth-talking Robinson, who stood behind her: "Miss Bella, love - give the young lady in front of you a chance. Let me enjoy the spectacle as you take her to bits. He gestured towards me. "But first, you. I would like to know your name and how you survived your exploits off the stern of one of my ships. Secondly I would like to *know what organisation you work for, before I allow Miss Bella to have her fun with you."*

So, playing for time, I told the story of how things had come about, but they still did not know too much - except that he was being stopped and the nuclear material was being recovered.

He laughed. "My ships are not vulnerable and you have not succeeded. I have all the fissionable material here and my weapon heads are ready to go to the Accelerator guns. Why? I hear you ask, before you die. Because I can! First the Jews will go and then I will have control of the world's oil fields. Nobody will do anything but bow to my needs. Where Hitler failed, I am and will succeed in taking over the world. You can't stop me and your employers don't know enough to follow you up. I know this as I have my people in every country's top secret organisation. Only because you are a private contractor have you got here, to the place where you will die! Go, Ciao - have your fun!"

Miss Bella came at me with a knife in her right hand, the blade forward from the little finger side, hand clenched in a fist around the hilt. Her right arm was held at chest height, with the blade pointing towards me. Her left arm was held at a similar height but with the palm open towards me. We circled for a short time. I had my little mushroom-shaped piece of hardwood in my right hand. Both my hands were up and forward at chest height, waiting for her first slashing, cutting lunge forward. We both inched sideways in a circular motion, neither of us blinking for an instant. I felt the sweat beginning to break out on my forehead and could see that she was drenched; she was not as fit as me and only used to easy prey.

She took a lunge forward and I sidestepped it to my left. She came again and I did the same; then once more. I was hoping she would recognise a pattern and would look for me to do the same. This time, as she came at me I went down onto my left leg, whipping my right leg around at knee height. She went down as intended; her hair was a mess by now and she began to get frustrated. That was one up to me!

The dance went on as Robinson laughed. Bella had now thrown her shoes away and was circling on the balls of her feet. A few more lunges came and I was *caught by one. Bella smiled as she saw the blood start to flow from my defensive left arm. The pain wasn't bad but the bleeding was enough to show me that fifteen minutes and I would be unconscious.*

Attack was now the only form of defence I had. As she came at me again, I went down and forward, rolling to my right and striking the outside line of her knee with the little wooden conch. Her left leg almost buckled as I slid past on the polished floor. She still grinned at me but she was starting to limp and the sweating was profuse. I knew I could win! This time, as she came in I jumped above the strike height and kicked the blade in her hand back at her. Her hand snapped back; the force had been enough for the hilt of the knife to take a front tooth out. That smartened her grin up!

We carried on playing tag and all the while the boys were getting on with their jobs. Soon enough I would hear the shrill whistle to let me know I had three minutes to get out of the complex. I had to keep fighting! The door I had come in through was still closed; I had heard two explosions which I presumed Berty had set off but they had failed to open the aperture. It was kill or be killed.

In this control room, only I knew our time constraints. I needed to step up a gear. Glancing around, I could see nothing that I could use to gain an advantage. I was going to have to bring her in and take the risk. I let her believe I was slowing and her lunges were getter better. On her last lunge, I pretended to slip, allowing myself to go down and roll onto my back. Naturally she followed, sprawling over me, expecting to draw the blade across my throat from left to right. As she did so, I placed my right arm out wide to look as if I was out of balance. Bella's face came close enough; moving fast, I whipped up my right arm and succeeded in slamming the conch into her left temple. She went slack and was out for the count.

I rolled out from under her with her knife and threw it at Robinson, who was already on his way out of another exit. He had heard the whistle and understood its meaning. I chased after him, but he had already gone down a series of tunnels. Several opportunities presented themselves to turn either right or left. I ran, not conscious of the bleeding arm but eventually I had to slow; I could feel myself losing consciousness.

I came round to find Berty lying over me, protecting me from debris that was falling around us. Missing the explosion, I had no idea as to the outcome of our attack. Knowing a little of my predicament and wanting to be my side, he had eventually got that damned door open. He had seen Ciao Bella laid out on the floor and left her to follow me as I chased Robinson as best I could.

We heard engines whining into life. Berty helped me get up and together, bleeding and dazed, we headed towards the noise. Entering into an area within a cavern, we found that we were standing a small jetty. A doorway that we had not discovered during our reconnaissance had, it appeared, been dropped below the waterline. We could see no vessel leaving and it left us puzzled.

That was that. We sat and hugged; I cried, knowing now that we had failed. Unless Robinson had been stopped somehow by someone else, the hunt would have to start all over again. We had won the battle but the war with this man was only going to go on. Exhausted, tired and low on blood, I collapsed once more.

Chapter 24: Endgame

The next thing I was aware of was that I was on board the submarine. The wound on my arm had been stitched and bandaged. Fluids were being dripped into me. Berty and my boys were all in the infirmary with me, with the exception of Alex. He had gone out and back to his wife Pat and was settling on the island for a well-deserved rest. All the SAS boys had got out and were on their way home. The sub would drop us at Gibraltar and it was there that Beetle and Jack would debrief us.

It ran in the usual fashion: lots of questions and some answers.

Robinson's centre of operations had been flattened, as had the Accelerator gun.

Although there was radioactive residue, no uranium had been found and it could only be assumed that he had not been ready to set off his economic revolution, or to start World War III at that particular time. He had obviously been very, very close to it!

The low-flying machine that he had escaped in was a new development being tested as far as the West were concerned but we now knew it was operational for the Red State. It could fly over water at up to three hundred knots, only twelve feet above the water. It had a very short wing span, gaining extra lift by forcing the air under the wings to hit the water surface hard. Robinson probably escaped with the uranium and could be anywhere within a thousand mile radius. He had probably headed towards the Black or Caspian Seas to lick his wounds.

All the countries that we had been acting for would be trying to locate Robinson. In the meantime it would be impossible to freeze his Swiss accounts and we could only presume he would surface at some point.

Charles and Berty would return to a life of normality, as would I. Erich was heading back to Switzerland to resume his normal employment and we would have to see how this all panned out. Alex would be paid enough to retire if he chose and spend some quality time with Pat.

Disappointed, bruised and wounded, I wondered when we would get to meet Robinson again. Would I be good enough to finish the job next time?

Norman Brown of Acklam and his wife were arrested for false accounting, spying and treason. They were probably hanged after being questioned; I never heard of a trial being held.

JJ settled and carried on working for Peter. She married and became Mrs. Brian Kuzman; I know she made him happy, as he did her.

Peter carried on with his business and later started to gain and retain genuine government contracts for highly technical work. His business also helped Berty and Charles with the production of specialised items when requested. Peter became a solid and good friend again after the embarrassment had died down.

The Times and Mr. Fleming took a slightly different view towards my employment, which looks like it will make a difference to my duties, as it were!

Beetle still had not found out what had happened to his boys, and just as MI5 did, he had all his Secret Service boys made aware that uranium was missing. They would need to be on the lookout for Robinson; the French, Israelis and all the others were going to be on the ball.

Robinson's shipping line was ceased and the ships broken up. His shareholdings in oil companies and drilling sites were slowly bled back into the markets, as if it had never happened. The captives that were still alive on his vessels were resettled at home with a pay-off that was to help compensate for their misery. Those who had lost husbands and sons were also compensated.

The Joint venture between the British and Soviet governments went on-line in

1954 as the first full commercial nuclear power station. It was just one hundred miles away from Moscow. Relationships from East to West and West to East were changing; the design became the standard for future nuclear power stations.

But the Americans had beaten us all at Oakridge, Tennessee by generating electricity using a heat source from a nuclear reactor on September 3rd, 1948.

Printed in Great Britain
by Amazon